the Cake the Wolf and the Witch

Maudie Smith

the Cake the Wolf and the Witch

Illustrated by
Tony Ross

Orion
Children's Books

First published in Great Britain in 2015
by Orion Children's Books
An imprint of Hachette Children's Group
a division of Hodder and Stoughton Ltd
Carmelite House
50 Victoria Embankment
London EC4Y 0DZ
A Hachette UK Company

1 3 5 7 9 10 8 6 4 2

The paper and board used in this paperback are natural
recyclable products made from wood grown in sustainable forests.
The manufacturing processes conform to the environmental
regulations of the country of origin.

A catalogue record for this book
is available from the British Library.

ISBN 978 1 4440 1 560 7

Typeset by Input Data Services Ltd, Bridgwater, Somerset

Printed and bound by CPI Group (UK) Ltd, Croydon, CR0 4YY

www.orionchildrensbooks.com

To Jenny Glencross, for her part in the quest.

ৡ⁓ Chapter One ⁓ৡ

"I'm not going in there. Not in a million years!"

Max stared in horror at the massive cake. It had five white tiers, all of them covered in frilly pink ribbons and creamy-yellow swirly stuff. It looked ridiculous.

But that wasn't the main problem.

Even without the trolley it was sitting on, the cake was much taller than Max. Now that it was on wheels, it towered over him, rising up towards the chandelier in the middle of the reception area. There was a stepladder propped against it, which they would have to use to get inside. Just looking at the stepladder made Max feel queasy. How had this happened to him? Why had Dad agreed to this cake thing in the first place? He knew how much Max hated heights, even low ones.

1

"I'm not doing it, Dad. I can't!"

But Dad couldn't hear. Everyone was clapping and cheering as he and Ilona made their way back into the hotel, huddled together under a big umbrella. The ceremony in the garden must have ended at last. Max hadn't stayed for the whole thing. He couldn't see the point of being out there, getting soaked, listening to drippy poems. He'd sneaked off and found the cake waiting for him by the kitchen doors. Like a fancily dressed dalek.

"This is the happiest day ever!" Ilona said in her sing-song voice. She was wrapped so tightly round Dad he could hardly walk, but he didn't seem to mind. He kept stepping on her long skirt and grinning at everybody.

"Dad!" Max called across the hall. "I'm not going in this cake, OK? It's stupid."

"Congratulations, Chris!" A big man Max didn't know took Dad's hand and pumped it up and down. "Great to see you looking so happy after all this time!"

Max turned away and put a foot on the bottom step of the ladder. Had anyone even checked to see if it was safe? Who was supposed to be in charge?

Dad and Ilona were leading the way into the dining room, with the chattering guests pressing in after them.

"Dad," Max called. "Get your inhaler out. There's loads of flowers on all the tables. They could be the ones you're allergic to." But Dad was being swept away from him.

As the guests streamed past, Max stayed where he was, crushing the flowers on his dandelion crown. It didn't matter if he spoiled it, because there was no way he was going to put it on his head. He'd agreed to the short trousers that puffed out over his knees. He'd agreed to the yellow cape Ilona had picked out for him. He'd even let her attach it to his shirt with the sparkly pin, which he was pretty sure was a lady's brooch. But no number of promises of equipment to build a brand-new marble run could persuade him to wear a crown made of flowers. He looked stupid enough as it was. It was lucky he hadn't invited anyone from school to the wedding. He could just imagine the expressions on Tony and Rio's faces if he had.

Suddenly Ilona unravelled herself from Dad. She wove her way back through the crowd of guests and rushed straight towards Max, arms outstretched, long sleeves flapping. He braced himself. It was too late to make a run for it.

"There you are, Max! Don't you look fabulous in those knickerbockers? I knew you would!"

He made himself go rigid while she hugged him. Ilona was always hugging him. It was quite alarming.

"Isn't this *lovely*?" She took a step back but kept hold of his shoulders so he couldn't move away. "I'm *so* pleased you let me marry your dad, Max, and we're all going to be together. Now we can all live happily ever after, can't we?"

Max didn't reply. He was too busy fighting with his face

3

to make it stay straight. What Ilona had just said was wrong on so many levels. Firstly, there was nothing lovely about the wedding, in his opinion. Secondly, he hadn't *let* Dad marry her – Dad had gone his own way on that. And thirdly, if they were all going to be together then there was absolutely no way that he, for one, was going to live happily ever after. Happy endings were for stories; they had nothing to do with real life. No one knew that better than Max.

"So, Max. How do you like our *grand gateau*?"

"Your what?" Ilona was always throwing bits of foreign languages into conversation. Dad said it was because of the travelling she'd done.

"The big cake!"

"Oh, that," Max said. "Well, actually, Ilona, the thing is—"

"Isn't it gorgeous?" Ilona pressed her palms together as if she was praying. "Your dad's such a clever carpenter!"

She reached up and tapped the fake icing on the lid.

"And when you little people burst out of it at the end of the speeches and surprise everybody, it's going to be absolutely *magnifica*!"

She looked at him seriously for a moment, her eyebrows up in her fringe.

"You can remember your line, darling, can't you?"

Max could remember it. All too well. He and the other two were supposed to pop up out of the cake and say, "Here's

4

to our very own happy ending!" He wished he could forget.

"Wouldn't you rather have a real cake? An edible one, I mean." Max hadn't been to many weddings but he thought the guests might be a bit disappointed if they were expecting something decent to eat, and all they got was a big wooden cake with three children inside.

Ilona darted forward and planted a wet kiss on the top of his head. It felt like someone had cracked an egg into his hair. "You're so sweet, Max!" she said. "I could just eat you up!"

He watched as she scurried away again, holding up the soggy hem of her skirt, her high heels clacking on the wooden floor. Max didn't exactly hate Ilona, but he really wished she'd stop saying such stupid things. He wished she'd stop pretending life was some sort of story.

No one was looking, so he tossed his dandelion crown into the bowl of sweets on the reception desk. He grabbed a handful of the sweets and shoved them in his right pocket. He already had his marble net in the left one. That was the only good thing about the knickerbocker trousers. They had decent pockets so he had a place to stow the marbles. He never went anywhere without them.

"It's in here," said a voice from the kitchen.

Max swung round to see Nettle, slouching against the ovens, staring at him. She was holding out one finger for Wild to hold on to, as he twirled in front of her.

It was bad enough that Dad was getting married again, forcing Max to leave his cosy flat forever and go and live in the new house Dad and Ilona were buying together. Worse still, he was going to have to break up the marble run he'd spent the past three years building. But worst of all, he was going to have to live with two bonkers children with totally bonkers names. Who called their children things like *Nettle* and *Wild*? Alarming Ilona, that was who.

And they were as weird as their names, he thought, as he stared back at Nettle. She was ten, just like him, but that was the only thing they had in common. They'd been thrust together in the same room several times to Get To Know One Another, but they'd never had a proper conversation. Nettle always glared at him when he arrived. Then she stomped about with her arms folded, flicking her messy hair, staring out of the windows and sighing, as if she was in prison. There was no way Max could talk to her so he always took the latest copy of *Construction Matters* magazine when they were forced to meet up. He'd read it for the entire length of the session, paying special attention to the section on Drains and Gutters, collecting new ideas for his marble run.

It wasn't always easy to concentrate on the magazine because Wild was forever asking him questions.

"What's your best colour, Maxi? Mine's red!"

"Maxi, what's your best job? Mine's baseball champion!"

"What's your best food, Maxi? Mine's gravy!"

Wild didn't seem to mind if Max answered the questions or not; he just kept trying to get on his lap and smiling, and staring into his face. Max wasn't used to little children and didn't know how to respond, but Nettle usually yanked Wild away before he had to try.

"It's in here," Nettle said again, pushing up the crown of leaves that sat on her knotty hair. She still hadn't bothered to brush it, Max noticed, not even for the wedding.

"What is?"

"The real cake." Nettle nodded towards a yellowish paving slab covered in orange sludge. "It's saffron and pine-nut."

"With satsuma icing," added Wild.

"Oh," Max said. Trust Ilona to come up with a disgusting flavour like that. "Why couldn't they just have a normal cake, with chocolate, or raisins?"

Nettle scowled. She had extra-thick eyebrows which made her very good at scowling. She seemed to have had a lot of practice, too. If there was a job going in scowling, Nettle would probably get it.

"Me and Wild baked that cake. It's an old Italian recipe. It's our present to Ilona and Chris."

"Right." Max thought it might be best to change the subject. He wanted to ask why Nettle always called her mum Ilona. Why couldn't she call her "Mum" like everyone else? But Nettle was still scowling at him and he doubted that

7

question would go down well. He decided to try something safer.

"I like your . . . outfit. Did you get it in town?"

The scowl turned to a glare. "Since when did the shops start selling suits made of real leaves?" Rustling crossly, Nettle let go of Wild and folded her arms across her chest. "Ilona made it. I'm supposed to represent Nature. But I look like a yeti."

"'Lona made mine too," said Wild. "I'm a little birdie." He slipped dizzily to the floor and a few feathers fell off the shiny silver nightie he was wearing. He smiled up at Max from under the brim of his red baseball hat. "I wouldn't take my hat off, though! I never take my hat off. Not even to go to bed!"

"Nature and birdie?" Miserable as he was, Max felt a snigger bubbling up inside him.

Nettle stared hard at the star-shaped brooch on his cape. "Yes. And you're supposed to be the sun. Coming out on our lives."

That sent the snigger right back down again, reminding Max there was nothing funny about any of this. He didn't understand this family Dad was making him join. They were a puzzle, and not the fun sort. Max liked the puzzles in *Construction Matters*. They were logical and he could work them out easily, but he didn't think he'd ever figure these people out.

"Time to get in the cake, kids." A lanky waiter wandered in, rolling up his sleeves. "They're about to start on the toasts. It's your big moment. Better get up that ladder!"

No, there was nothing funny about it at all.

Chapter Two

Wild galloped ahead, into the hall.

"Cake time, Maxi-Nettle!"

He seemed to enjoy lumping their names together like that. He seemed to think it was funny. Max wished he wouldn't do it. It sounded as if he and Nettle were one person. Which they weren't. They were totally different, to look at and everything. Nettle was taller than him, and dark-skinned, with loads of curly hair and strong arms. Whereas he had straight fair hair, and although he wasn't a massive wimp like Tony and Rio sometimes said, he was a bit on the skinny side.

"Up you go, guys," said the waiter.

Nettle sighed and tramped her way easily up the ladder. Max noticed she was wearing the same chunky boots she always wore, although they had been covered with some sort of moss for the occasion. She jumped down inside the cake.

Wild clambered after her, quick as a monkey.

"Wheee! I'm flying!" he whooped as the waiter reached up and swung him over to Nettle.

"Now you, mate."

Max hovered anxiously at the bottom of the stepladder, clutching his marble net in his pocket.

"Max! What are you waiting for?" Nettle leaned out of the cake. "Hurry up. I want to get this over with."

"Give me a minute," Max said. "I've never done anything like this before."

"First time for everything then, isn't there," Nettle replied, not very kindly.

"I don't see why there has to be," Max muttered. It was easy for her to say. Max couldn't even stand on a chair without feeling that he was about to fall. He couldn't tell Nettle that, though. She'd probably laugh at him. He'd never seen her laugh but he reckoned it would be even harder to take than the scowling. He took a firm hold of the sides of the stepladder. It was only seven steps. He could manage seven steps, couldn't he? And this was what Dad wanted. He'd do it for Dad. He started to climb, counting each step as he went.

"You might want to open your eyes for this bit," the waiter said when he reached the sixth step.

11

He let his eyes open a crack. Everything was whirling. He felt dizzy. His hands were so slippery he could hardly hold the ladder. He tried to wipe the sweat off on his cape but that made him wobble and he grabbed at the ladder, rocking it violently.

"Hey! Careful!" said the waiter. It was too late. Max fell, tumbling straight into the cake. He cried out as he landed heavily, upside down on a piano stool. Someone must have put it there for them to sit on.

"Idiot!" Nettle hissed.

Max rubbed his shoulder.

"Made a bit of a meal of that, didn't you?" The waiter's face appeared above them. He was holding the lid of the cake.

"Do you have to put that on?" Max said.

"'Course. Can't let you go without your icing, can I?"

"Can you at least leave a gap, so we can breathe?"

The waiter lifted the cake lid higher. "Sorry. Orders is orders. Fasten your seatbelts, ladies and gentlemen. You're in for a bumpy ride!"

"What seatbelts?" Max looked round in a panic.

"Oh, for heaven's sake!" Nettle rolled her eyes. "It's a joke. We're only going to be wheeled from here to the dining room. You don't need a seatbelt for that."

She scratched at her stomach. The leaf suit looked pretty itchy. Max might have felt a bit sorry for her if she hadn't said, "What is it with you? Are you afraid of *everything*?"

Her words were like stings. Nettle was definitely the right name for her.

"I don't like risks, OK?" he snapped back. "What's wrong with that?" He was suddenly afraid he might have a panic attack. He'd had a few of those before. He'd started having them after Mum's accident. They made him feel like he was drowning.

"Have fun, guys!" The waiter clamped the lid over them, giving it a slap to make sure it was securely fixed.

"Ooh, dark!" said Wild. He sounded as happy as Max was miserable.

Max hated dark places at the best of times, and this wasn't the best of times. Far from it. He felt very uncomfortable squashed between Wild on one side and Nettle on the other. Wild smelled a bit farty, as if he needed the toilet. Max hoped he was potty-trained. And Nettle's mossy boots were pressing painfully on his feet. He only had on the silly slippers Ilona had chosen. They were all soft, like ballet pumps. That was another reason he was glad he hadn't asked Tony and Rio. They would have called him a girl.

There were loads of people at this wedding, almost a hundred. Two of them were jammed up right next to him, but Max had never felt so lonely in his life. He missed Mum more than ever today.

He needed his marble net. He hoped he hadn't dropped

it in the fall. With a bit of manoeuvring he managed to put a hand in his pocket, but he got a shock when he realised there was another hand in there already. A little, sticky one, closed right round the marbles.

"What's these, Maxi?"

"Give them back!" Max shouted. "You give them back!"

He grabbed the marbles out of Wild's hand but must have caught his elbow on his chin or something because the little kid yelped.

"What's going on?" Nettle demanded in the dark. "Did you just hit my little brother?"

"It was an accident!" Max insisted. "He took my marbles."

"What marbles? What are you talking about?"

"I only wanted to look at them!" Wild piped.

"Well, you should ask first." Max tucked the marbles as deep in his pocket as possible. "I've kept these marbles in perfect condition for three years, and you just swipe them. Pickpocketing's a crime, you know!"

"Oh, shut up, Max!" Nettle said. "They're only marbles." He could imagine her rolling her eyes as she reached across him. "You OK, Wild? Don't worry about Max. He's being an idiot."

"Don't mind," Wild said with a sniffle. "Sorry, Maxi. You can have my crayon if you like. It's my favourite. I bit the top off but it still works."

"No thanks. It's all right."

Max did his best to turn away. He hadn't meant to hurt Wild and he knew he wasn't really a pickpocket. If it had been anything other than his marbles it wouldn't have mattered at all, but he couldn't explain that now.

He squeezed the net in his hand, and the marbles inside clicked together reassuringly. Nettle said they were only marbles. But they weren't. They were the most important marbles ever. Mum had given them to him just before she went on her expedition. That was the last time he'd seen her. He'd never opened the marble net: he was saving it for when his marble run was finished. He took it everywhere with him.

"Stop fidgeting," Nettle told him. "What's the matter with you now?"

"Nothing. I don't like small spaces, that's all!"

"Well, why did your dad build this cake for you to go in, then?"

"I don't know. Because your mum told him to, probably!"

"Chris and Ilona in love!" announced Wild, as if that was an answer to anything.

Max still didn't understand it. How could Dad have fallen in love with someone else? It was three years since Mum had died, but it had never crossed his mind that Dad might get married again. It had taken him ages even to realise that Ilona was Dad's girlfriend, and not just a friend. And if he had imagined Dad marrying, he would have expected him to choose someone who looked, or at least behaved, a bit like Mum. Mum was sensible and practical and she dressed nice and tidily. Ilona wore floaty dresses and had loads of long hair that sometimes trailed into her soup. She was nothing like Mum. Max really didn't want to live with Ilona. Or Nettle, or Wild. He wished this whole wedding thing would go away. He wished he could just go home and be on his own in his room, with his marble run. Working on the run was his favourite thing. He loved designing extensions to it, checking and rechecking his measurements, cutting bits of wood to the exact length required, making each new addition perfect. When he was concentrating on that he was all right. He didn't need to think about anything else.

He knocked on the roof of the cake.

"Why aren't we going anywhere yet? I want to get out!"

"All right, eager beavers," came the muffled voice of the waiter. "You're on!"

The cake started to move. Max felt the wheels rattling and scraping beneath him as they rolled along the floor. He clutched his marble net. Panic was rising up through his chest and he was panting a bit.

"Calm down, Max!" Nettle said sourly. "You'll be out in a second and then we can all get on with having our very own happy ending!"

Suddenly Max forgot about being anxious and got incredibly cross instead.

"That is so flipping stupid!" he shouted. "There is no way we're all going to live happily ever after. Your mum might believe in happy endings but I don't. There is no such thing as a happy ending! And I know. As a matter of fact, *I'm an expert!*"

As he finished speaking, the cake suddenly lurched and went completely out of control. It began to spin and to jerk, like a fairground waltzer.

"What's going on?" Max yelled.

Before anyone could answer he felt the cake rear up, tipping them backwards on the piano stool. Then it lifted right off the ground.

Max screamed as the cake rocketed upwards into the air, with the three of them jammed inside.

"Make it stop, make it stop!"

Max chanted the words through gritted teeth. The cake was spinning so fast the back of his head seemed to have welded itself to its flimsy walls.

"Whee! Funny, Maxi-Nettle! Funny!" Max could feel Wild rocking backwards and forwards by his side.

Max couldn't even lift his head. He felt sick.

"What's going o-on?" His voice was wobbling. So was the cake, as if it was a jelly being buffeted about by strong winds. "What's ha-appening?"

Without warning, the cake plunged downwards. Max shrieked with terror. They were all going to crash and die!

Wild squealed with delight and clapped his hands.

"More! More!"

He was only four. He didn't understand what was going on. Then again, neither did Max. Nettle was completely silent. Max couldn't see her in the dark but he was dimly aware of her body, tensed up next to his.

Air whistled around them. Max felt as if he'd left his stomach hundreds of metres above him. He was getting further away from it with every heartbeat.

He was wondering how many heartbeats he had left when there was a deafening roar, like powerful aeroplane brakes. The cake hit something hard, bounced three times and then scudded along the ground, before finally coming to an abrupt halt. The piano stool slammed into the front of the cake, and then the back. He heard Nettle say, "Oof!" as she fell off the stool.

And then nothing.

Max had no idea what had just happened, but whatever it was, it was over. He sat very still, clutching his marble net, thinking what a wonderful thing stillness was.

"Yay!" said Wild. "Again!"

There was no other sound at all. Max was glad not to have roaring in his ears any longer, but things seemed so quiet. Too quiet.

"Nettle?"

"What?" she murmured.

He was quite relieved when she answered. He'd begun to think she might have been knocked unconscious.

"Are we in the dining room, do you think?" If they were, he ought to be able to hear the wedding guests. They'd all been chatting like mad earlier. "Is this when we're supposed to pop out and say the line?"

"Not sure." Nettle sounded dazed. "We could try it, I suppose."

"Go on, then," said Max.

"OK. You first."

"Why? What are you worried about?"

"What are *you* worried about?"

Max couldn't explain it but, much as he wanted to escape from the dark, enclosed space, he was still anxious about lifting the lid.

"Don't worry, Maxi-Nettle," Wild chirruped. "I go first!" Max felt him clamber onto his shoulders.

"Wait, Wild," Nettle said, but the lid of the cake slid away. Daylight shot in. It was so bright Max had to shield his eyes.

"Woweee!" Wild said, hanging onto the rim of the cake and scratching his head through his baseball cap. "Pretty!"

Before the wedding ceremony, Ilona had covered all the tablecloths in blue and yellow flowers and hung streamers from the light shades. That must be what Wild was looking at, Max thought.

"Ready, then?" he said to Nettle, who was shielding her eyes too. "Let's get this over with, shall we?"

"All right."

Max cleared his throat. He hoped Dad appreciated what this was costing him, standing up in front of all these people and saying something he didn't believe one little bit.

Together, he and Nettle stepped onto the piano stool and popped their heads up out of the cake.

"Here's to our very own happy—"

They stopped.

There was no one there.

No Dad, no Ilona, no wedding guests. There were no lights strung with fancy decorations. No tablecloths. No tables. There was no hotel dining room.

There wasn't even a hotel.

Chapter Three

"Dad?" Max said. "Are you out here?"

"Ilona?" said Nettle.

No one answered.

"Birdies!" said Wild, smiling up at a pair of red birds floating in the sky.

Max remembered looking up at the sky when Dad and Ilona had kissed during the wedding ceremony. It had been full of rain clouds. Now it was powdery blue and dotted with white cotton-wool clouds. The lemon-yellow sun was surrounded by bright rays, like cartwheel spokes, that looked as if they'd been painted onto the sky.

"What's going on?" Nettle said. "What's all that?" She was looking across a carpet of thick green grass at some very unusual trees. Their branches were entirely symmetrical.

Each tree looked exactly like its neighbour. Glancing round, Max saw that they were surrounded by more matching trees.

"Are they fake?" Nettle asked. "Did your dad make those as well as the cake?"

"Of course not."

The trees were too perfect to be real, but Dad could never have made so many. They were all linked together, as if they were holding hands. Some of them even seemed to have faces.

"Maybe they've hired some scenery," Max said. "But why would they do that? Why didn't they tell us about it?"

"Maybe they wanted it to be a surprise." Nettle seemed as baffled as he was.

"My dad doesn't do surprises." Although now that Max thought about it, Dad had changed quite a lot since he'd met Ilona. Maybe he *would* do something like that, if she wanted him to.

"OK, we're surprised. You can come out now, Dad. Well done. Very funny."

Nothing happened. Max hadn't really expected it to. Deep down he knew there was no way Dad could have organised so much scenery. He just wished he had, because then Dad could pop out and say "Surprise!" and clear things up. What on earth was going on?

Nettle frowned at the strange landscape, picking leaves off her suit. "Something's not right about this," she said.

"I know. Dad!" Max called. "Where are you?" He felt panicky. The place was so quiet and still, and there was nothing he recognised.

"Ooh, bunnies!" Wild pulled himself up over the rim of the cake and tumbled right out onto the bright green grass. He rolled down the slope towards a group of brown rabbits, gathered in front of a clump of big bushes. They lolloped away, their perfectly round white tails bobbing. Wild laughed and lolloped after them. He wasn't a bit worried, Max noticed.

"Wait, Wild!" Nettle called as Wild disappeared into the bushes. "Wild! Get back here!"

She looked as puzzled about their surroundings as Max was. She was starting to climb out of the cake when an adult's voice said, "Do not be afraid. I have Wild."

Max looked around, trying to see who was speaking.

"The child is quite safe."

The voice was coming from among the bushes. Max peered towards them, hoping whoever was in there would explain what was going on, or at least direct them back to the hotel dining room.

"Hello, big doggie!" Max heard Wild say. The person he was with laughed. Max thought maybe it was the waiter, although it didn't sound much like him.

"Wild!" Nettle shouted again, just as the little boy reappeared. He was hopping along next to a tall figure, who

23

was leading him back up the slope towards them. It wasn't the waiter, though. Very definitely not.

Max stood for a moment, not sure whether to believe his eyes. Then he screamed and flung himself backwards. As his head thudded into the wall of the cake he realised what the problem must be. He was suffering from concussion. He must have banged his head during the cake ride. And it must have been one heck of a bang to make him see what he was seeing now.

Because Wild was trotting over the grass towards them, holding hands – or rather, paws – with a wolf.

"Good day to you, Max. Nettle."

A talking wolf.

"Thank you very much for coming."

A tall, slightly mangy, bushy-tailed, walking on its hind legs, fully dressed, speaking English as if it had done so all its life, *wolf*!

"A pleasure to meet you both," said the wolf, resting an arm – or rather, a front leg – on the rim of the cake.

As Max pressed himself backwards, a musky smell of damp fur met his nostrils. He knew concussion could make you hallucinate. Could it create imaginary smells too?

"Look what a nice big dog I found, Maxi-Nettle," Wild said proudly.

"Come over here, Wild," Nettle said, reaching out of the cake towards him.

"Why?" Wild looked reluctant to let go of the paw that enclosed his tiny hand.

"Because that's . . ." Nettle spoke slowly, keeping her voice steady, "that's not a dog. It's a wolf."

Max was dismayed to realise that Nettle was seeing exactly what he was seeing. That meant he couldn't be concussed after all, not unless she was concussed too, in exactly the same way as him.

"Fear not, Nettle," the wolf said. "I mean you no harm."

"How . . . how did you know our names?"

That was just one of many questions Nettle might have asked. At least she could speak, Max thought. He was having trouble even breathing. He hated it when things didn't have rational explanations, or got out of control. Whatever was going on here was completely out of his comfort zone.

He tried to look closer, to see if the wolf was really a man dressed in a wolf suit. But if it was a dressing-up outfit, it was a very good one. He couldn't see any zips or fastenings, and the whole thing was very lifelike. Especially the head, with its shining eyes and lolling tongue, and the jaws full of jagged teeth. And that smell.

"I've been expecting you," said the wolf. "I'm so glad you could join us here. I hope you had a smooth journey."

"Not particularly," Nettle said. "And where is *here* exactly?" She seemed to be trying to keep the wolf's attention while still beckoning furiously to Wild to drop its paw and come to her.

"I'm sorry," said the wolf. "I'm forgetting my manners, am I not?" It stood back and bowed to them. Wild made a grab for its tail, which was sticking up out of the waistband of its baggy green trousers. He caught it in both hands and brushed the fluffy bluish plume across his forehead. He giggled. "Tickly tickly!" he said.

"Wild!" Nettle hissed.

The wolf laughed. "Don't give it a second thought," it said, as if Nettle was concerned about Wild being rude rather than the terrible danger he was in. The wolf stood up straight and spread its paws out wide.

"Welcome, friends. Welcome to Happy End! Follow me, if you please."

"What did it just say?" Max whispered as the wolf led Wild away towards a gap in the trees.

"Follow me, if you please," Nettle mouthed.

"No, not that. The bit before. What's Happy End?"

"Oh my gosh!" Nettle's hands flew to her mouth. "It's taking Wild!"

She scrambled out of the cake. "Come on," she said, staggering to her feet. "Quick! Get out of the cake!"

Max didn't move.

"Max! What are you waiting for?"

"To wake up."

"What?"

"Yes," he said, relieved to have thought of a logical explanation. "This is obviously just a dream and I'm going to wake up from it in about one minute." He wasn't concussed. He must be having a dream. A very vivid, lifelike dream. It had to be that, because if it wasn't, Wild had just disappeared through the gap in the trees with a real live wolf. And that was totally impossible.

"What are you talking about?" said Nettle, her voice rising anxiously. "If it's a dream, how come I'm having it too?"

"You're not. It's my dream. You just happen to be in it, that's all."

Nettle started walking quickly towards the trees. "Stop wasting time, Max. Are you coming or not?"

"Not." Max sat back down in the cake. "Definitely not." He didn't need to go, because none of this was real. He could just wait here until he woke up.

"Idiot!" Nettle yelled as she broke into a run. She vanished into the trees. Soon he couldn't even hear the thumping of her moss-covered boots.

"Idiot, yourself," Max said, to fill the silence she'd left behind.

It felt peculiar being on his own in the cake. And it was eerily quiet. It was only a dream, of course, but he still didn't like it. He decided to think about his marble run. That's what he usually did when he wanted to take his mind off things. It might steer the dream in a better direction.

He'd been working on the marble run for almost three years now. He'd started it just after Mum had died. When it was finished, he planned to open Mum's marbles at last, and let them go down it. He was going to have to do that soon, now he and Dad were moving out of their flat, but the marble run still wasn't quite ready. He hummed quietly to himself, remembering the smooth, evenly spaced dips in which the marbles would wait their turn at the top of the run. He liked to let his mind go zooming down the slides and over the ramps, through all the pipes and tunnels he'd ever built. Finally, he loved to imagine the two up-ended scooter wheels round which the marbles would do a double loop-the-loop before coming to rest at the end of the track. The loop-the-loop was his favourite bit of the whole run.

Thinking about the marble run wasn't as calming as it usually was. Max couldn't concentrate on it at all. He really should have woken up by now. What if he *wasn't* dreaming? How had they got to this place? He tried peering over the edge of the cake into the trees. Was the hotel through there somewhere? Maybe the cake had some kind of hidden engine. Had it got out of the waiter's control and brought them outside by accident?

"Hello? Dad! Where are you?"

There was no answer, but the trees shivered and shook. A

sudden sharp breeze lifted green leaves from their branches, whipping them into the air and blowing them in circles around Max and the cake. The wind ruffled his cape and he felt his neck go cold, as if an icy hand had rested on it.

He whirled round.

There was no one there. But he had a creepy feeling, as if someone he couldn't see was watching him. The wind had died down as suddenly as it had begun but the sky, which had been so blue a moment before, was dull, and the lemon sun had faded to a more watery yellow. Long, fingery shadows appeared as if from nowhere and rippled over the ground like snakes. Max fancied he could hear the grass sighing uneasily as they passed through.

Max shivered. Even if this whole thing was a dream, he didn't want to be left on his own in it any longer.

He clambered hurriedly out of the cake, glanced around one more time, then straightened his cape and dashed for the gap in the trees.

Chapter Four

There was a single path winding ahead of him. Max raced along it. As he ran, rabbits scattered away into the bluebells. Above him, woodpeckers in the trees paused in their drilling. A pair of deer, grazing in the sun-dappled grass, raised their heads and twitched their ears, staring at him with glossy brown eyes.

He still wasn't sure what was going on but he had to admit everything seemed very real and he didn't *feel* as if he was dreaming. Maybe these were the hotel grounds, but if so, they were a lot bigger than he'd thought. He couldn't see Nettle and Wild anywhere. He ought to have caught up with them by now. He didn't fancy being lost out here on his own so he ran faster, bursting out of the woods into a large, open garden.

The path was grassy now and lined with neat flowerbeds. Max rounded a strongly scented rose bush in full flower, and was very relieved to see a tall lady with a bow and arrow. She was practising archery in the middle of a lawn. Maybe archery was an activity laid on by the hotel. If so, she would know the way back to the main entrance. He ran towards her. He'd soon get things sorted out.

"Excuse me," he began. He was about to ask for directions to the hotel reception when he realised she was just a statue. Her stony fingers stayed fixed to her bow and her lifeless gaze passed straight over him and stretched far across the lawn.

"Oh!" Max's hopes fell, but as he turned away, he caught sight of a boy dressed in brown, disappearing behind a clipped hedge. The boy was very small, even smaller than Wild, and he had his hands up in the air as if someone was pointing a gun at him, although as far as Max could see there was no one about apart from him and the lady statue.

"Hey!" Max called. "Wait! Have you seen a girl in a leaf jacket and a little boy in a nightie, by any—"

But the boy didn't even turn round. He just yelled, "You can't catch me!" and ran off chuckling, with his hands up.

"Charming," Max muttered. What was so important that the boy couldn't stop to give directions to someone who was lost?

He hurried on past a pond full of lily pads. An extra-large

frog croaked and did an elegant dive into the water. Max couldn't remember seeing a pond before, but he decided he must really be in the hotel grounds. That was the only simple explanation for all of this. It still didn't explain the wolf, but maybe he'd just imagined that. Yes, he told himself, that was it. The wolf had simply been a figment of his imagination.

He came to a curved flight of stone steps, ran down them three at a time, and stopped.

Who was he trying to kid?

The wolf was there again. Large as life.

It was standing on a wide terrace, its paws clasped behind its back, talking quietly to Nettle and Wild. The three of them were staring at what could only be described as an amazing palace. A palace with balconies and flags and a million windows. A palace which, unfortunately, looked nothing like the Greenacre Hotel in Mansley.

"Ah, Max," said the wolf, turning back the cuffs of its silky orange shirt. "You've caught up with us. Doing some research of your own back there, were you?"

"Huh?" was all Max could think to say back. Research? The only thing Max was interested in researching was the way back to the hotel.

"Bill's showing us round," said Nettle. Astonishingly, she and the wolf now seemed to be on first-name terms. Max didn't think it was a good idea to call the wolf by a name, especially an ordinary name like Bill – that made it seem

32

far too normal. He had no intention of calling the wolf anything.

Nettle seemed calmer now but she was looking rather pale, Max noticed, as if she'd just been told some bad news and was struggling to take it in. Max knew what that felt like.

"Are you OK?" he said, but she didn't answer.

Wild tugged at the wolf's trousers. "Wild wants a carry, Bill," he said.

The wolf picked the little boy up, curling a claw around him. Max winced at the sharpness of the claw, imagining it piercing Wild's skin. He looked at Nettle. She ought to be trying to get Wild away from the wolf but all she was doing was staring numbly at the palace.

"Shall we?" The wolf gestured towards the palace with his free paw.

"It looks like the Sleeping Beauty palace," Nettle said, gazing at the flags drooping down above them, "before the vines grew up it."

"After they came down, in fact," said the wolf. "Although I'm afraid it is suffering from wear and tear once again." He picked at a hole in the palace wall and yellowy dust showered out of it. "Aurora and Casper are most concerned."

"Who? What are you talking about? What's happened to the hotel?" Max couldn't stand this. Not knowing what was going on was making him all jittery. "Where's Mansley?"

33

The wolf turned towards him, stroking his muzzle with one paw as if something was puzzling him.

"This way, if you will, Max. There are some people I'd like you to meet."

"No, please. I don't want to meet anyone. I just want to go home!"

He'd told himself before the wedding that all he had to do was be there, say the happy ending line and then keep his head down until it was all over. He'd just about been prepared for that but he certainly wasn't ready for this. Whatever it was.

But the wolf was already padding purposefully up the palace steps, with Wild perched in his arms. He gestured for Nettle to go ahead of him through the huge studded doors. She did so, and the wolf, bending his head to miss the red roses that climbed around the doors, went after her.

Miserably, Max followed them. The wolf must have knocked the roses because petals fell like confetti onto his shoulders. Oddly, they weren't red but grey. It crossed Max's mind that he'd never seen grey flowers before.

He was still brushing petals from his cape when he found himself in an enormous hall with red and white marble floors and tall swirling pillars. It was a much grander place than the hotel – or it had been once. Cracks spread like rivers through the marble floor. The huge portraits that hung from the walls were skewed, and their subjects, kings and queens by the look of them, all had worried expressions on their faces. They looked as anxious as Max felt. The gigantic chandelier in the centre of the ceiling made the one in the hotel reception look like a toy, but it wasn't too stable, Max noticed. It was hanging from a frayed rope. He made a mental note not to stand directly underneath it.

A group of people in fancy-dress costumes were gathered in the hall, arguing in loud voices. They all stopped talking immediately when they saw the wolf.

"Well, Bill Fairfoul." A tall snooty-looking girl in a golden dressing gown addressed the wolf. "Which one of them is it? Have they brought equipment? When can they start?" She looked the three of them up and down, quite rudely, Max thought. She seemed vaguely familiar, although he couldn't remember meeting anyone like her before.

"Don't be so impatient, Aurora," said a much smaller girl, in a red cape and hood. She looked familiar too, like someone he knew from a long time ago. "Just because you're royalty doesn't mean you can snap your fingers and make things happen right away. They've had a long journey. At least give them a chance to say hello."

"You're Red Ridey Hood!" Wild told the girl.

"Spot on, shrimp," said the girl. "I'm Red. And this is my gran." She pointed to an elderly lady with a lacy nightcap and wire-framed glasses.

"Have a bun, dear?" the old lady said. The wolf let Wild down to the floor and he went over and took two buns from the plate she offered him.

"Yummy yummy," he said, smiling at her as he munched.

Then it clicked. That was it! All these people, Max realised, were dressed up as characters from stories. Somehow, he and Nettle and Wild must have stumbled into some old country house. And this was a dress rehearsal for a play. That would explain why this Bill person was dressed as a wolf. He'd need to take a better look at him – he must have Velcro or poppers on him somewhere after all.

A teenage boy, wearing a velvet hat with a large feather in it, rushed over to the girl in the dressing gown. "Sorry I'm late, my love."

"Oh," he said, his eyes widening at Max and Nettle and Wild. "They've come. Gosh! Are they going to be up to the job, do you think?"

What job? He was about to ask what the teenager meant, when another boy, in climbing gear rather like Max's mum used to wear, sauntered to the front of the group.

"Doubt they will be," he said with a sneer. "None of Bill Fairfoul's other ideas have worked, so why should this?"

"My thoughts exactly, Jack," said a freckly-faced woman at his elbow. "They don't look like no experts to me, son."

Max didn't like the way these people were looking at him, and he had no idea what was going on. A muttering began, which suggested that whatever the woman was talking about, most of the others agreed with her.

"Why should we trust the wolf, anyway?" the girl they were calling Aurora said. "Don't you think it's a bit odd, him turning up out of nowhere just after Lord Malberry disappeared? How do we know he's really on our side?"

"That's right," said Jack's mother. "He could be working for Babs Haggard for all we know. I mean to say," she gestured towards Red Riding Hood, "wolves don't exactly have a great reputation round here, do they?"

This made so little sense to Max that he thought they must be saying the lines from the play. He tried to catch Nettle's eye to see if she agreed, but she was listening intently to the conversation.

"Well, he's not *my* wolf," Red said. "I don't know where Bill Fairfoul came from, any more than the rest of you do, but the wolf in my story is dead. My dad slit him through from end to end. There's no way *that* wolf's coming back."

"He might, though," Aurora said. "The way things are, we don't know what might happen. Things might come back, evil things, even things we thought were dead."

A worried silence fell. If these people were actors, Max thought, they were very convincing ones. Aurora's words sent shivers up his back.

"Look here, folks. None of us has got any better ideas,"

Aurora's boyfriend said at last. "So at least let's give it a chance. Which one of them is it, Bill?"

"Thank you, Prince Casper." The wolf, Max saw, still looked worryingly lifelike. He had been waiting patiently through all this, apparently picking real fleas from his fur. Now he came directly towards Max and, before he could duck out of the way, put two heavy paws on his shoulders.

"May I introduce Max. Our Happy Ending Expert."

"*What* did you say?" Max spluttered and backed away into a pillar. If there was one thing he was still quite sure about, it was that whatever was going on here, none of it had anything to do with him.

"You said it yourself," the wolf carried on. "I saw you in the Pool of Portent. You said you were an expert. That's why we brought you here to Happy End. We need your help."

"Happy End? What's Happy End? What's a pool of portent?" Max turned to Nettle, who was standing very still, staring at all the people ranged in front of her. "What is this? This is some kind of pantomime rehearsal, right? It's just a made-up play." His voice shook. He didn't really believe it but it was the only halfway logical explanation he had left, and he so wanted it to be true.

His heart sank as Nettle shook her head slowly.

"No, Max. It isn't a play. It's real. Bill just told me. We're in some kind of story world. It's called—"

"The Land of Ever After!" Wild sang, spinning round on the spot.

"Yes," Nettle said. "And this is Happy End. It's the capital, apparently."

"*What?*" Max couldn't believe what he was hearing. He shook his head. "No. That's not possible."

"Not possible," Nettle said. "But happening." She pointed at Aurora. "That's Sleeping Beauty, and this is her palace."

"No!" Max stared at Aurora. Was that really why she looked familiar, because he'd seen her in an old book of fairy tales? Like the one Mum used to read to him?

"Story! Story!" Wild yelled. "Hello, Jack Beanstalk." He grinned up at the boy in climbing gear. "You sold your mummy's cow!"

"Let's not go there again," Jack said, glancing at his mother. "I don't want it all coming back to haunt me."

"We don't want any more truck with giants," his mother said, her eyes large and frightened. "No. We're done with all that, thank you very much."

As she spoke a gust of wind blew into the palace, tinkling the chandelier, rippling through everyone's clothes.

"It's happening again!" Red cried. The wind flapped her apron, and it turned quite suddenly from red to grey.

"My crown!" Aurora screamed, clutching at the little tiara perched delicately on her head. A moment ago it had been sparkling and golden. Now it was dreary and dull.

39

A tray of goblets flew into the air, dropped and smashed on the marble floor. Dust showered down from the ceiling and the chandelier swung as if it was threatening to fall.

"Babs Haggard," Max heard people murmur. "It's happening more often too. That's three times today." He could tell they weren't acting now. They were genuinely afraid, and as the things they were saying began to sink in, he felt afraid too.

"What's going on?" Nettle said, picking up a dull grey candlestick. "This was all silver and shiny a minute ago. That was like magic."

"It is magic," the wolf said. "The worst kind. It's Babs Haggard's magic, and she's getting stronger all the time."

"Who . . . who's Babs Haggard?" Max asked. He'd run out of all possible logical explanations now and was feeling so shaky, he wasn't sure he even wanted to hear the answer. No one seemed to want to give it to him either.

Finally Prince Casper whispered, "A mean and jealous soul."

"With ice and venom in her veins," Aurora added.

"The very essence of evil," Red's grandma put in.

And Red said simply, "A witch."

Max wished he hadn't asked. He didn't want to hear about witches. Especially not if they were real, as he was now very much afraid they might be. He flopped down on a velvety sofa and gazed at Wild, who was playing hopscotch, jumping from red marble tile to red marble tile. Max felt light-headed. He thought he was about to start hyperventilating because it was hard to catch his breath. He concentrated on breathing in and out slowly.

He was still dimly aware of the conversation continuing around him. The wolf and the others were all going on about someone called Lord Malberry. Apparently he was some sort of magical protector who until recently had been in charge of the whole of the Land of Ever After. But Lord Malberry had mysteriously disappeared. He'd announced he was going on a journey and would be back in a few days, then weeks had gone by and he hadn't returned. After his departure, everything had started going wrong. The people who lived in Happy End had stopped being happy and had begun falling out and squabbling. Not only that, but their beautiful world was starting to turn grey. Everything in it was crumbling too, as if it was slowly but surely dying. They said it was something to do with the witch called Babs Haggard. They seemed to think she had stolen Lord Malberry's magic. Some of them even thought she had killed him. The whole conversation was smattered with disturbing words like *destruction*, *evil* and *annihilation*.

Unable to take it all in, Max stared blankly ahead. He was vaguely aware of Wild, sliding through the dust in his socks towards the open doors at the back of the hall. As he drew near to them, a new freak wind swept in, rushed

41

over Wild and lifted his baseball cap right off his head. Wild made a grab for it but missed. The cap hovered above him for a moment, almost as if it was daring him to try again, and then flew out of the door.

Wild slipped straight out after it. Max lost sight of him for a moment, but he soon reappeared, scrambling up some smooth stone slabs, snatching at the hat as he went. He probably shouldn't be wandering off on his own like that. Max was just thinking that he ought to tell Nettle what had happened when his view was blocked by the tall body of the wolf, and all thoughts of Wild went clean out of his head.

". . . and that's where you come in, Max."

"What?" Max blinked up at the wolf.

"Max! Have you been listening to a word Bill's been saying?" Nettle demanded. "You've got to go on a quest."

"Me?" He'd been hoping that if he kept quiet, the wolf might forget all about him.

"Yes, you." Nettle rolled her eyes. "Amazingly."

"Yes," said the wolf. "Max will go on a quest to Beyond. He will find the witch and overcome her. He will restore order and bring back happiness to Happy End. Max will save our world."

"Wait. Please!" Max was so confused. Why were they all looking at him?

"How long has he got, do you reckon?" said Red Riding Hood.

"I don't know," said the wolf, "but our sun is beginning to fade, and judging from the destruction Babs Haggard has already wrought, I fear we have no more than three days left. Max is our last chance."

"What do you mean?" Max said. "A quest? To Beyond? What's that?"

"It's a long way off," said Jack. "On the other side of Harsh Mountain."

"Harsh Mountain?" Max wasn't keen on anything he'd heard so far, but he really didn't like the sound of Harsh Mountain. He didn't like mountains at all.

"No one can tell you what Beyond is like, though," Aurora said with a sniff. "Because no one who's been there has ever come back."

"You'll be the first." Jack nodded at Max. "If you make it."

As Max began to understand what was being asked of him, a feeling of dread filled his stomach. He couldn't go off on a mission to a place that no one had ever come back from and start fighting an evil witch. He wasn't that sort of boy at all. He was a boy who had panic attacks, who only left the safety of his flat when he was forced to. He had absolutely no idea how to stage a rescue or find lost magic. How *did* you go about defeating a witch?

"No, look, sorry, but I really think you've got the wrong person." He tried to laugh. "I mean, you're having a joke, aren't you?"

He scanned all their faces but no one looked as if they found anything remotely funny.

He tried again. "You see, when I said I was an expert, back in the cake, I didn't actually *mean* it. And I'm not sure what your Pool of Portent thingy is, but I think it must have had some kind of data error." He had to make them understand. "I'm not a superhero or anything."

"You can say that again," Nettle commented – rather unnecessarily, Max thought.

"Why does it have to be me, anyway?" he said to her. "Why can't you do it?"

"Because I'm not the chosen one, am I?" she snapped. "I'm not the expert!" She plopped down on a velvet couch and hugged her knees. Everyone else was still staring at him.

"But . . . can't you do it yourselves?" He knew he sounded desperate, and he was – desperate to get home.

"Alas, no." The wolf prowled about as he spoke. "It has long been written that if ever Babs Haggard were to tip the balance and turn goodness into evil, only a child from the Other World would be able to overcome her power. Now that Lord Malberry is gone, she is at large, extracting all the colour and light from our land, spreading meanness and hopelessness as if it were a disease. Make no mistake, that witch intends to erase every happy ending that ever existed. I believe it is her intention to bring back all the unhappy endings instead. Babs Haggard is gaining power and she will not rest until she rules the whole of Ever After with her rod of evil and despair. Only a child can defeat her and restore order to our land. And it has to be the right child. The chosen one."

He stopped prowling and faced Max.

"The Pool of Portent never makes mistakes. That child, Max, is you."

"But," Max stammered. "No. I mean, I'm sorry about your troubles and everything, but I can't help you. And even if I could, I've got to get back. My dad. There are these flowers on the tables. I need to tell him to use his inhaler. Ilona won't remember. So, do you think you could get the cake, please, and send me back where I came from? It's the Greenacre Hotel in Mansley."

He sounded as if he was talking to a taxi driver but he knew he wasn't. He knew he was talking to a real wolf. He knew they weren't actors. He believed it all now. He even believed in the existence of the witch. And because he believed it, he was all the more anxious to get out of here, and to get home. He looked pleadingly at Bill Fairfoul.

"I'm sorry." The wolf studied his paws sadly, as if he understood some of what Max was feeling. "That won't be possible. When Lord Malberry departed, he took his magic with him. A very small amount was left behind. He may have left it for emergencies. We used it to bring you here."

Max gulped. "All of it?"

"Every last drop," confirmed Red.

"Great!" Nettle said under her breath. "Now we're all stuck here."

"Yeah, bright idea of yours, wasn't it, tufty features?" Jack said.

Bill Fairfoul ignored him and looked Max straight in the eye.

"I'm sorry, Max, but we couldn't send you home now, even if we wanted to."

Chapter Five

"Oh!"

Max let out a sob and suddenly found himself fighting back tears. He'd never been apart from Dad since Mum had died, except to go to school. He hardly ever went to other people's houses, not even for tea. He and Dad took care of each other. They had to. Especially since it was just the two of them. They couldn't risk any more accidents, not after what happened to Mum. "There's a whole world out there," Mum used to say, but Max wasn't interested in seeing the world. He just wanted to be with Dad. Dad was all he had. And Max was all Dad had too – or he had been, until Ilona came along.

He felt his voice breaking as he said, "I can't do this. I can't. I really, really need to go home!"

"Don't be a wimp, Max!" Nettle said, sounding sharper and more prickly than ever. "Pull yourself together, and go and do the quest. Go to Beyond or wherever it is and bring back the magic. And hurry up, please. Because none of us can go home until you do. Have you even thought about that? Me and Wild shouldn't be here at all. We're only here because you said that stupid 'expert' thing in the cake."

"Don't make it my fault," Max retaliated. "The cake was Ilona's idea. Not mine. And I never said I was the sort of expert they mean. I've been badly misunderstood." It was more than a misunderstanding, he thought. It was a disaster.

Nettle tossed her hair. "You're so busy feeling sorry for yourself, aren't you, Max? But what about us? What about me and Wild?"

Max was just about to say that it was all right for them, they weren't the ones being asked to fight a witch, when Nettle said, "Wait. Where *is* Wild? Where's my little brother?"

The story characters seemed puzzled. "He was here a moment ago," Prince Casper said, peering round a pillar. Jack searched behind the sofa, Red pulled back the curtains, and Aurora checked her voluminous skirt as if she thought Wild might be under there, playing hide and seek.

"Wild!" Nettle called. "Wild! Where are you?"

"I know where he is," Max said, suddenly remembering. "He went out of the back doors. After his hat."

48

"What?" said Nettle. "He went outside? On his own?"

"Yes. He headed up those grey slabs." He'd meant to say so as soon as Wild left but he'd been in such a daze and there was so much going on, it had slipped his mind.

"Oh my goodness gracious!" exclaimed Red's grandma, pressing a hand to her mouth. "Don't tell me he's gone over Giant Fell!"

Everyone gathered round the window and stared out.

"That's terrible."

"That's not safe!"

"Not safe?" Nettle said. "Why not? Let's get after him, then! Someone show me the way."

She rushed to the doors but no one joined her. The story characters shuffled about uneasily.

They wouldn't meet her eye. Wild could have gone quite far by now, Max thought. He wished he'd mentioned it before.

"What are you all waiting for?" Nettle demanded.

"Sorry, love. But we daren't go out," Jack's mother admitted at last, twisting a leather bangle on her wrist. "It's Babs Haggard, you see. This is the safest place there is at the moment."

"It's not even all that safe here," Red added as some plaster dropped from a pillar and scattered on the floor at her feet.

"It's much more dangerous out in the open," said Aurora. "We're not leaving the palace, I'm afraid."

"But he's only *four*!" Nettle said.

Still no one moved to help her.

"Honestly! You lot might be afraid of going outside, but I'm not. I'm going after my baby brother." Nettle stormed out of the doors.

Max watched with everyone else as she ran down the slope and climbed the grey slabs. He felt a bit responsible and thought he probably ought to go with her, but she hadn't actually asked him to go. Besides, he told himself, Nettle would get along much faster than he would have done. He wouldn't be able to run in his silly wedding shoes.

"She'll catch up with him in a second, I should think," he said to no one in particular. It was awkward, being the only person from the real world in a palace full of story people. He coughed and straightened his cape. *Construction Matters* was tucked in the lining. He'd put it there earlier, just in case there was a boring bit at the wedding. He was pleased to see it. His brain was so muddled, he really needed a break. He could read the magazine until Nettle came back with Wild. He flicked through for the Gutters and Drains section, and started to hum.

He'd hardly begun reading when a claw punctured the paper in front of his nose. Max gasped as a pair of deep, bronze-coloured eyes bored into his.

"Aren't you going to help your sister?"

"My sister? Oh, Nettle's not my—" He stopped. He

supposed that, since the wedding ceremony, Nettle *was* sort of his sister now. It had only been that way for about half an hour, though. And she didn't behave like a sister. Why should he help her, especially when she was so horrible to him all the time?

But the wolf was looking at him in such a disappointed and disapproving fashion that he felt instantly guilty. He put down the magazine and stood up.

"Well, all right. I'll go and meet them. I expect they're on their way back now anyway, don't you think?" No one answered. "See you back here in a minute, then," he said, trying to sound cheery. Again, no one spoke, so he backed out of the palace. He tripped over the step, righted himself and stumbled away.

He'd be as quick as he could. The others had said it wasn't safe outside. He wasn't quite sure why but he scurried along, keeping as low as possible, just in case.

Giant Fell was a pretty funny name for a hill. And it was a pretty unusual hill. The first part of it was grey and smooth and stony, whereas the next was soft and pink and a bit spongy. At least it wasn't too steep, Max thought, leaping up onto some long green logs. He balanced his way along the length of them, jumping down onto a wider expanse of pink.

"Nettle?" he called. "Wi-ild! Where are you?" He hurried on, and the pink, soft land was replaced with brown earth, dotted with coarse clumps of short black grass.

He called their names again but there was no reply. He went faster, glancing around for signs of Nettle or Wild. He wasn't fond of Nettle but she and Wild were the only real people in this entire place. The three of them probably ought to stay close.

"Aagh!"

His foot went down a hole and he fell forward, jarring his chest on a pointed bit of rock. He grabbed onto a clump of wiry grass, next to a dark pool of water, and pushed himself up awkwardly.

Then he shrieked.

What he had taken for a pool of water was an enormous, staring eye. An eye as big as a Frisbee. And the grass he was clinging to wasn't grass at all. It was eyelashes.

"Oh!" he cried out as he let go.

It wasn't brown earth he was lying on. It was a face. The face of a huge, lying-down giant. The green logs he had run along weren't logs, they were great big runner beans, sticking out of the giant's shirt pocket. Without realising it, he'd just run the entire length of an actual giant's body. And as if that wasn't bad enough, his foot was now caught in a giant's mouth!

Now he knew why the hill was called Giant Fell. The great figure beneath him must be Jack's giant, lying exactly where he'd fallen.

Max scrambled to his knees, struggling to free himself.

"Help!"

He wrenched his leg desperately, dragging his foot out of the hole. His ankle hurt and was bleeding. He'd cut it on the giant's huge teeth. It looked like quite a bad cut too, but he couldn't stop to examine it now.

He hopped over the giant's eyes and up into its shaggy hair, hanging onto big brown locks as he scrabbled his way down. He landed in fleshy green stuff, like enormous rhubarb leaves. Wading through it, he guessed it must be the remains of the beanstalk, the one that Jack had grown.

The beanstalk itself was thick as a handrail. Still in shock, Max used it to haul himself away, dripping blood onto the leaves as he staggered along. He remembered what the story characters had said about Babs Haggard changing all the happy endings to unhappy ones. He hoped the giant wasn't suddenly going to wake up and smell his blood, the blood of an Englishman! This place might be made up of nothing but stories, but they were stories real enough to do actual harm. His bleeding ankle was proof of that.

He was looking back, checking the giant wasn't stirring, when he heard a giggle. It was coming from inside a small copse of trees ahead of him. The trees weren't like the perfect green ones he'd seen before. They had thin, spindly, white trunks. Max glanced up and was reassured to see the trunks were joined to branches, branches which had silvery leaves. They really were trees, not the legs of some enormous fairytale ponies. He was swiftly coming to the conclusion that you couldn't take anything for granted round here.

A second, familiar giggle told him he'd found Wild. Nettle was probably already with him. He began working his way through the trees. They'd get Wild and take him back to the palace. Nettle should tell Wild off too, for running away. He could have got himself into real trouble. They'd have to go round the giant this time, of course. Max definitely wasn't going over him again, but they'd get back to the palace somehow and sort things out. What the wolf had said about all the magic having disappeared from Happy End was a mistake. It had to be. They'd get the cake working again and go back to the hotel. Thanks to *Construction Matters*, Max knew quite a bit about engineering. He might even be able to help.

He reached the bottom of the slope and peered round the last tree into a clearing.

In it was the most enormous red toffee apple Max had ever seen in his life. It was practically the size of a small car. It was upside down with its flat end on the ground. Its stick reached upwards like a flagpole. Hanging on the very top of the stick was Wild's baseball cap.

And Wild was there. There was no sign of Nettle. She must have gone the wrong way.

Wild was sticky and a bit red, as if he had been licking the side of the toffee apple, but right now he was concentrating on his cap. He was climbing some steps at the edge of the apple. Only they weren't steps, Max realised, but three big pink mice that looked to be made of sugar.

"Thank you, Mr Mousie," Wild said to the topmost mouse. He stood, teetering, on its head, then clambered onto the upturned apple. The mouse didn't blink. It couldn't have blinked, even if it had wanted to, Max saw. None of the mice had eyes, just hollowed out spaces where their eyes ought to go.

He was about to shout at Wild to come down when the little boy suddenly started to shin up the stick of the toffee apple. "Stay there, Wild's hat!" he said, and chuckled. Max couldn't shout now. He knew you should never distract someone who was climbing without a rope. Mum had told him that. He'd just have to wait for him to come down. Then he'd go straight over and get him.

Just as Wild's fingers touched the hat, the toffee apple suddenly reared up off the ground and bucked him high into the air. It all happened so quickly, Wild couldn't have had much idea what was happening, but as he fell he managed to grab the top of the toffee apple stick and cling to it with his arms and legs.

Max watched, horrified, as a thick black liquid, like tar, surged up from the ground. It swept over the apple, coating it, blotting out its jolly red surface. The apple hissed and cracked and began to expand into a wide bowl shape.

The sugary mice, which had been so still, fell away. They bulged and swelled and turned yellow as old mustard, until they weren't mice any longer but hideous gnarled chicken feet, bigger than dogs. The chicken feet crept blindly around the black bowl, positioning themselves at three points beneath it as it came to rest on top of them. Now it looked worryingly like an enormous witch's cauldron.

No sooner did Max have time to think this, than a lid flew back off the bowl and a terrifying head came shooting out of it.

It was the head of a woman. A terrible woman. She looked half alive and half dead, maybe even three-quarters dead. Her hairline began way back on the pale dome of her head, and her hair, which was the colour of fresh bruises, was dragged upwards and held in place with long pointed skewers. Her cheekbones stuck out sharply and her eyes, which were much too big for her pinched, grey face, spun round in her head like two shiny black billiard balls.

Max was too terrified to move. His brain had room only for one appalling thought: this awful creature must be Babs Haggard. He was standing just a few metres from an actual, totally scary, properly evil witch!

He shrank back as the witch leaped upwards, a pair of sharp wings whirring on her back. Under her skirts were big furry feet with long claws which she hooked over the lip of the cauldron, steadying herself there. She opened her mouth, and Max saw a set of jagged teeth just like the ones on Dad's sharpest saw-blade, as she broke out a terrible smile.

"Crackle crackle!" she screeched. "Crackle crackle!"

Suddenly she grabbed a huge spoon out of her cauldron and poked it upwards, pushing Wild's tiny hands off the toffee apple stick. He fell down in his feathered nightie, a winged bird.

"Come to your Auntie Babs, my darling," the witch croaked as he dropped into her arms. She wrapped long, rake-like hands around his body.

Wild didn't speak. He stared up at her, his mouth frozen in an O shape, his eyes wide with shock.

"Are you the best they could do? You're nothing but a babe in the wood!" the witch sneered, and acid-green steam puffed from her mouth. "But I'm so pleased to see you," she hissed into Wild's face. "Because now my story is really starting. We're cooking at last, aren't we, my little crackling? Now we'll see who's going to live happily ever after!" She squeezed Wild with her skeletal fingers. "Crackle crackle!"

And she laughed. It was a deafening laugh, full of screaming winds. It pierced Max's body, making him double over in pain.

"Away!" The witch swivelled her black eyes and beat the chicken feet with her spoon. "Back to Beyond!"

Clutching his stomach, Max stared as the chicken feet clawed at the ground with their gnarled talons. They lumbered up under the weight of the cauldron, which began to spin, throwing up clouds of dust, whirring loudly like a helicopter about to take off.

"No! Wild! No!"

Chapter Six

"Wild! Wild!"

For a moment, Max wondered if he was shouting the words himself, but then Nettle came sprinting through the trees.

"Wild! Wild!" she yelled, about to pass Max and charge into the clearing.

"No! Wait!" Without thinking, Max lunged and grabbed her round the waist. They both fell to the ground.

"Get off me!" Nettle struggled but Max hung on to her leg.

"Don't! She'll see you! She'll catch us all!"

Wild must have heard them because he twisted his head round in their direction. His high little voice rose over the thrumming noise of the cauldron. "Maxi-Nettle! Help, Maxi-Nettle!"

"HAAALT!" the witch screamed at the chicken feet as if she was addressing a small army.

Max and Nettle both froze as the thrumming slowed. Babs Haggard threw Wild up in her arms and caught him again, holding him against her chest, facing out, as if he was some sort of trophy. She revolved slowly in the cauldron, her heartless black eyes rotating in their sockets.

"Maxi-Nettle, is it?" she said, a weird, bent smile on her hideous face. "Maxi-Nettle."

Max kept totally still. Had she seen them? If not, he expected Nettle to shout and give them away at any moment – but now even she seemed stunned into silence.

Babs Haggard couldn't have seen them, though. She nodded and seemed satisfied. She dropped Wild into the cauldron, pressing him down out of sight, and she beat the chicken feet again.

"On, on!" she shrieked.

The spinning sped up. The chicken feet careered away, swaying beneath the rolling weight of the cauldron. It crashed through the trees like a chariot, branches withering and falling as soon as it touched them.

In a matter of moments the cauldron, the witch, and Wild were gone.

Max was so scared, he didn't want to move ever again. He might have lain where he was forever if Nettle hadn't got up and kicked his shins.

"Ow!" He reeled away from her. "What did you do that for?"

"For stopping me from saving my baby brother!"

"But I saved *you*." Max rubbed at the lump already swelling on his leg. "If I hadn't pulled you back that witch would have caught you too. I did you a favour."

"You did it to save yourself. I hate you, Max! You're a selfish, useless coward!"

"Well, where were you? You should have got here before me. If you'd been a bit quicker this never would have happened!"

"I slipped, didn't I? Into that giant's armpit. It took me ages to climb out." She came towards him again, fists raised.

"Enough!" a voice commanded. They both turned to see the wolf looking down at them. He was at the top of the tree-lined slope, standing on the outstretched fingers of the fallen giant.

"No fighting, I beg you."

"He deserves it!" Nettle spat. "He held me back." Max could tell she would have attacked him again if the wolf hadn't asked her not to. Bill Fairfoul was mangy and smelly, but there was something about him, a quietness, a sureness, that made people listen to everything he said. Max had noticed it in the palace. Jack and the others were suspicious as to his identity, but they still seemed to respect him somehow.

61

"Where is Wild?" the wolf asked. "Did you find him?"

"Yes. But I was too late. The witch took him. He's been kidnapped!" Nettle choked back angry, frightened tears.

"This is grave indeed," the wolf said. "But, Nettle, your quarrel is not with Max. It's with Babs Haggard."

Nettle let her hands drop to her sides, as fear replaced the anger in her dark eyes. "What will she do to him?"

Max followed her gaze through the dark hollow left by the witch's cauldron-chariot and he remembered the look of sheer bewilderment on Wild's face when the witch had caught him.

"She won't hurt him, will she?" he said. Wild was so little. No one could possibly want to hurt him, Max thought. Not even a witch.

Bill Fairfoul looked very serious. "That I don't know. But if she suspects Wild is the chosen child then you may be sure she wishes him no good. And an innocent such as Wild is a great prize for someone like her. His capture will give fuel to her cause." He clapped his paws together. "You must leave at once. You two will work together now. You will be company for one another on the journey to Beyond."

"Company!" Nettle spat the word out as if it tasted bad. Max turned his back on her to show he wasn't exactly delighted either.

The wolf watched them calmly.

"But first, we must deal with your injury, Max."

Max had completely forgotten about his cut, but looking down he saw that his left slipper was soggy with the blood which still seeped from his ankle.

The wolf signalled for Max to join him on the giant's hand. Max hesitated. Had he just seen the giant's fingers twitch? But the wolf waved a paw. "This fellow's story ended a long time ago. He cannot hurt you. He can't hurt anyone. At least, not at present."

"Do you mean he might wake up?" Max didn't feel like going anywhere near the giant again. "His story might start all over again? And end . . . differently?"

"That is why you are here, Max, to see that it doesn't. Now come."

The wolf cupped his two paws together. "May I?"

"OK, then."

Cautiously Max put out his leg and the wolf took it in his paws. He opened his jaws, his tongue lolling out, and breathed over Max's ankle. The rank smell of the wolf's breath alone was probably enough to make the cut go septic. Max grimaced and turned his face away to where Nettle was crouching, angrily retying her boot laces.

"That's better," the wolf said softly.

Max looked back at his ankle. The cut had gone: the skin was smooth and intact. There was no sign that anything had ever been wrong with it. It didn't even hurt.

"How did you do that?"

The wolf's eyes gleamed. "I do possess a little healing magic," he said. "I inherited it from my father." He straightened his back. "Now you are ready to go."

"But . . . " Max let his eyes follow the path the witch had taken. He didn't *feel* ready to go. He didn't think he ever would. "I'm not brave."

"But you will be. Believe me, Max, it's no mistake that you are here."

Nettle snorted in disgust. She swept at the ground with one foot, like a pony impatient to gallop.

"And no mistake that you are here, Nettle, either. You will play your part in this, just as Max will." Max felt the wolf's glittering eyes on him again. "You do accept the quest now, don't you, Max?"

Max nodded. Every bit of him still wanted to refuse the quest but he knew he couldn't, especially not now that Wild had been kidnapped. Unless he defeated Babs Haggard and found Lord Malberry's magic, there was no way any of them would ever get home.

"You couldn't come with us, could you?" He'd been scared of him at first but now he thought he'd feel a lot better with the wolf at his side.

Bill Fairfoul never smiled – presumably wolves couldn't – but at that moment he looked as if he might like to. "I wish I could, but I must remain at the palace. I have vowed to protect Happy End and will do so for as long as I am able." He wiped a weary paw over his ears. "Or for as long as Happy End exists. We cannot delay any longer. The Land of Ever After is running out of time."

As if to prove it, the giant let out a long, moaning sigh. Max and Nettle both shrank back but Bill Fairfoul didn't move.

"How long have we got?" Nettle asked.

The wolf glanced at the sun. It looked even paler than before. "Our sun is waning quickly," he said. "Now that the witch has Wild, I doubt it will have the strength to rise more than two more times."

Two days! It was an impossibly long time, and an impossibly short one too – especially, Max thought, if you hadn't the first idea what to do.

"We don't have a map," Nettle said. "We don't know the way."

"Go straight towards Harsh Mountain. And look for the Shining Pathway. That is the route you must take."

"What shining pathway?" said Max. "What's that?" How could the wolf be so sure?

But Bill Fairfoul only said, "Now hurry. Take care of one another, you two, and beware of Babs Haggard's agents. Remember, things are not always what they seem. And, I beg you," his bronze eyes glazed a little as he stared into the distant hills, "keep an eye out for poor lost souls."

Then he tore his gaze away. "Enough! I bid you farewell."

He bowed slightly, then loped off up the giant's forearm without looking back.

"Right!" Nettle said. "We've wasted enough time here. I'm going." She stomped away immediately, in the direction the witch had driven her cauldron.

Max stood for a moment. How could he possibly go on a quest in the state he was in? He had no one to help except a brand-new sister who hated him and wouldn't even wait for him. And the only equipment he had was his marble net, four slightly squashed sweets in shiny green and purple wrappers that he'd pinched from the hotel, and a chewed white wax crayon Wild must have put in his pocket when they were in the cake. He was completely unprepared for a quest, yet somehow he was going on one.

Swallowing his nerves as best he could, he straightened his cape and went the way Nettle had gone before him.

Chapter Seven

Max found himself walking parallel to a narrow stream, which trickled along its stony bed. It was dark under the trees. The sun, which had turned so pale, seemed to be having trouble penetrating the gaps in the branches. It gave so little light that he could only just see the tall, pinkish spires of flowers growing among the trees.

"Nettle?" he called quietly, not wanting to draw any unwanted attention to himself. This place looked normal enough, but who knew what might be hiding in the bushes? What if Babs Haggard had caught Nettle already? What if she'd seen him too and was lying in wait, about to leap out of the trees?

"Ne-ttle?"

He didn't like Nettle much but he'd much rather be with

her than on his own. He sped up a bit, and called louder. "Neee-ttle! Where are you? Nettle!"

The rippling water seemed to whisper his words back at him but there was no answering call from Nettle.

"This way. Not far now."

Max dived off the path as a crystal-clear voice he didn't recognise cut through the air.

He crouched down among the woodland flowers. There were people coming his way. Quite a lot of them, judging by the sound of tramping feet. He pressed himself lower, remembering the wolf's words about Babs Haggard's agents. He didn't want to meet any of those, especially not on his own. He held still and tried to control his breathing.

"Keep going, dear ones," another voice said. "We'll be at Happy End soon. We should be safe there."

Peeping between the flower spikes, Max glimpsed a young man and a young woman, walking arm in arm, leading some children along the path. The children were all dressed in capes with hoods so he couldn't see their faces as they passed. He counted seven of them. The people didn't look dangerous – they were probably just a family making for the safety of the palace – but he didn't want to take any chances. He stayed where he was for a few more moments, in case anyone else came by. He felt safer hidden by the flowers.

They were foxgloves, he realised. Foxgloves had been Mum's favourites. Most of them were a bright pinkish purple, but a few were grey, just like the roses he'd seen over the palace entrance. Max knew now that grey wasn't the flowers' natural colour. They were like that because of Babs Haggard. He felt a surge of anger squeeze in with his fear. What business did she have destroying the things other people loved? And if it hadn't been for her he'd probably be back at home by now, working on his marble run.

He knew he needed to find Nettle. If the witch hadn't caught her, she would be way ahead of him by now. He rejoined the path and started to walk fast, checking over his shoulder in case anyone was following him. The path was clear, for the moment. He walked faster, then broke into a run.

He was aware, as he ran, that the stream next to him was quickening and widening all the time. In a matter of minutes it had turned into a fast-flowing river.

Max stopped. The path ended abruptly next to a bridge. Quite a decent bridge too, like a sturdy camel hump. There were no other paths so Nettle must have gone over it. He started across, scanning the opposite bank. He thought he heard giggling coming from the trees on that side. Trying to trace the sound, he caught sight of movement among the leaves.

"Can't catch me!"

The little boy in brown he'd seen in the palace garden was there again. He still had his hands up in the air. Were they stuck like that? If so, it must be very uncomfortable.

"Run as fast as you can," he crowed in his tinny little voice. "You can't catch me!"

"Wait!" Max shouted. "Wait a minute!"

But the boy just giggled, ran on again and disappeared. It was as if he was teasing Max in some way. Why, though? What had Max ever done to him?

He was almost at the other side of the bridge when he ran straight into something large, soft and round, which bounced him backwards, knocking him down on the hard planks.

"Tilly wants her billy goat!"

"Wh-what?" Max looked up, but all he could see was a massive stomach, partly covered in a jumper made of thick string. Looking higher, past the jutting shelf of belly, he saw the hugest and most crumpled face ever.

The face came closer, knitting its hairy eyebrows together.

"Tilly wants her billy goat!"

"Who . . . who's . . . Tilly?" Max was so scared his teeth chattered. This was it. His quest was over, before it had even begun. This thing was going to kill him!

"I is Tilly. Tilly is me." The creature poked its own chest with a greenish and stubby thumb. "I is Tilly the bridge-keeper. And I wants my billy goat! Have you got one for me?"

"What? No! I—"

70

The creature took hold of Max's cape and lifted him up by it and shook him. He dangled helplessly, clutching at his throat. He didn't know which was worse – the fact that his cape was strangling him or the smell of old cabbage and rotting socks coming from the creature's armpit.

"You give me my billy goat," the creature demanded, "or else!" It raised a squishy green fist. "Tilly's waiting!"

Max could barely speak. A noise came out of his mouth which was meant to be the word "Please" but it came out as "Pleeeeeeeaaat!"

The creature squinted at him. "*You* isn't a billy goat, is you? You *is*! That's you bleating!"

Max squealed, suddenly sure he was about to be eaten. He wriggled and tried to tug his cape away from his neck, but it was throttling him, and he couldn't speak. "Naaahgil!"

The creature chuckled. "This is my lucky day," it said, swinging him about. "I've always wanted a billy goat and now I's got one."

Max closed his eyes and prepared to have his toes bitten off, or his fingers.

"Excuse me, miss!"

"Huh?"

The swinging halted, and Nettle appeared on the bridge, dripping wet and panting. For the first time in his life Max was pleased to see her.

71

"Excuse me, I'm sorry to interrupt, but the thing is, that isn't a billy goat you're holding. It's a boy."

"Boy?" repeated the creature, as if trying out the word for the first time. "Boy, is it?"

"Yes. And I'm a girl," Nettle added.

"But I don't need a boy. Or a girl. I needs a billy goat."

The pudgy hand opened and Max fell onto the bridge, coughing.

"Sorry," Nettle said, squeezing water from her leafy jacket. "I'm afraid we haven't got one of those."

The creature seemed very disappointed. "Oh. Well, what has you got then? You can't go crossing my bridge without paying, you knows. There's a toll."

"All right," Nettle said. "Max will give you something, won't you, Max?"

"Will I?" Max was still fighting to get his breath back.

"Yes. What about those?" Nettle put a toe on his marble net. It must have fallen out of his pocket when he was being swung. It was a miracle it hadn't fallen into the river. "Give those to the lady," Nettle said.

"No!" Max grabbed the marbles and tucked them away. It was weird, but even in this dire situation he wasn't willing to give up Mum's marbles. He searched his pockets for something else. Wild's chewed crayon was there, but that wasn't much of a present. Then he found the four sweets from the hotel. "You can have these if you like."

"Ooh! Jewels!" said the creature. She snatched the sweets and twizzled them around, smiling as the watery sunlight glinted on the coloured wrappers. "Tilly likes jewels!"

She pushed two of the sweets up her nostrils, and bunged the other two into her ears. "Tilly pretty!" She leaned over the bridge to see her reflection in the water. "Does I look pretty?"

"They're not actually for—" Max began, before Nettle trod on his hand.

"Very pretty," she said. "Lovely, in fact." Slowly she backed away. Max started to crawl after her on his hands and knees.

"Oh, no you don'ts!" A big foot landed on Max's back and he collapsed. "I isn't letting you go yet. I'm giving you a something in return."

"You don't need to do that," Nettle said. "Max doesn't want a something, do you, Max?"

"No!" Max shook his head vigorously. "Nothing. I'm fine." He lay on his front with the creature's big foot in the small of his back.

"Yes, I does need to do it." Tilly was firm. "If I doesn't give him a something in return, Boy might get the wrong idea. He might think he's paid for a return ticket when he hasn't." She scrabbled in a pocket on the front of her tatty, spotted swimming shorts.

"Here you are." She dropped a handful of hard and tiny bluish balls into Max's hand.

"Thanks," said Max. "They're . . . very nice."

Tilly grinned. "Now you can go," she announced. "Remember, though. One-way ticket only. And when you comes back, I wants a billy goat as payment, all right?"

"All right." Max got to his feet.

"Pinky promise?" The creature stuck out the biggest little finger Max had ever seen in his life.

He knew he couldn't possibly keep the promise. Where was he going to find a billy goat? But he put out his finger anyway. Gingerly he touched Tilly's enormous finger with his own.

"Pinky promise. A billy goat. Right. Thanks very much."

"Bye bye." Tilly waved wildly into their faces, even though they were still right next to her. Then, appearing to get bored, she ducked and disappeared under the bridge with a splash. "Seeeeee youuuuuuuu!" she called.

"Byeeee!" Max said faintly. He staggered over the bridge and scurried up into the forest after Nettle, glancing back over his shoulder to make sure Tilly the bridge-keeper wasn't following him. He shuddered, wondering what other terrifying creatures might be waiting for him on this dreadful quest. He wished he was back at the hotel. He'd hated being at the wedding but now he'd have given almost anything to be back there. He wouldn't mind being in the cake either.

He'd happily stay shut up inside it for hours, if only he could be there, and not here.

Nettle strode ahead through the trees, pushing at brambles that flicked backwards, some of them whacking into Max and scratching his arms and legs.

"Ow!" he said after the third time it happened. "Are you doing that on purpose?"

"What if I am? You deserve it. Getting yourself caught by a troll like that. It was obvious that was a troll's bridge. A baby could have seen it." She shook her wet hair. "That's why I swam across, upstream."

"That thing was a troll?" Max said. "Wow."

"Of course it was a troll. Don't you remember the Billy Goats Gruff? What use are you going to be in the Land of Ever After, Max, if you can't recognise a simple story?"

Max knew she was angry but she didn't have to be quite so nasty.

"I can't help it if I'm a bit rusty. It's a long time since I read a story."

He hadn't read one at all, he realised, since Mum died. They used to read together a lot, but after the accident he'd gone off books and stories completely. It was all right for Nettle. She would be up to date with stories because she had a little brother. At least, he *hoped* she still had a little brother. The image of Wild's astonished face when he was kidnapped came into his mind. He tried to think of something else.

"What are these things anyway?" he said, taking out the wrinkled blue balls the troll had given him, and rolling them around in his hand. "Some sort of magic beans? Like the ones Jack planted? I'm not going up any beanstalks. I don't like climbing."

"I know that," Nettle said. "It was obvious from the fuss you made getting into the cake. You'd never know your mum was a climber. You are such a weed!"

Max kicked at a pebble. There was no need for her to talk to him in such a hurtful way. "You sound like Tony and Rio."

He'd started tagging along with Tony and Rio soon after Mum had died. He'd spent a lot of time on his own at first, but then they'd sort of scooped him up and given him parts to play in their games. They were quite nice to him most of the time, but not when he wouldn't do the daring things, like walking on the school wall, or swinging on the rope in Rio's garden. Then they always said he was a weed, and he would go off and sit on his own with *Construction Matters*, and wait for Dad to pick him up. Now, if they ever did manage to get home he'd have Nettle there, calling him names as well. That was all he needed.

Nettle swung round. "Who are Tony and Rio? Do they go to your school?"

She'd never asked him a question about himself before. He was so surprised, he just nodded.

She signalled to him to open his hand so she could examine Tilly's gift.

"Juniper berries," she said, as if she was rewarding him for the information.

"How do you know?"

"I know a lot about cooking." She walked away again. "I collect recipes when we're travelling. I've got different ones for every country. Juniper berries aren't edible when they're raw, but they add flavour to stews and stocks, and casseroles."

The berries were totally useless as far as Max could see. He brushed them back into his pocket as a thought occurred to him. Nettle had got him away from Tilly all right, but now, thanks to her, they were burdened with another impossible task.

"I don't know why you had to promise her a billy goat," he said. "Where are we going to find one of those?"

He trod on her heels as she stopped abruptly in front of him.

They were in a field. A field which led to another field, and after that another. The fields stretched away for miles. In the distance Max saw a range of lumpy hills. Behind them rose a sharply pointed mountain, black, and capped with snow or ice. His heart lurched. That must be Harsh

Mountain. How was he, of all people, supposed to climb that? Even if they reached it in one piece, they'd never get over it.

Nettle had gone very pale and he guessed she was thinking the same thing. Her lips set in a thin line as she turned to him. "So what do we do, Max?"

"What?" Nettle obviously despised him. He hadn't expected her to consult him.

"Yes. What's your plan? How are you going to get to Beyond in time to save Wild and the Land of Ever After?"

"I . . . well . . . I . . . " He knew he had to do it but he had no idea how. The wolf hadn't explained that. "I suppose we should just . . . keep going."

"Brilliant!" Nettle spat. "I could have told you that!" She stormed ahead again. "I'd be a million times better off on my own!" She glared back at him. "And you're so slow!"

She was being really unfair, Max thought, as he tried to keep up with her in his silly slippers.

"I did say I wasn't the right person for the job," he said. "I don't know how to run a quest. I never said I could do it. I can't!"

"Well, for some unknown reason," Nettle said as she marched on, "Bill Fairfoul thinks you can. He thinks you have it in you to save this world. So it would be handy if you could start doing something about it. You should be making plans and devising strategies." She flashed angry eyes back at him. "When are you going to do that, Max? When are you going to do something positive? When are you going to stop being a complete and total waste of space!"

And as if that wasn't mean enough, she turned and gave him an almighty shove in the chest, which sent him flying. He landed hard on the grass.

He sat up, winded. He was about to protest when an enormous white horse charged by, thundering over the very patch of ground on which he had been standing just a moment before.

"Whooaaaaah!"

The horse skidded to a halt and reared up, whinnying, eyes rolling.

Its rider, a burly knight in a full suit of silvery armour, clutching a very long, sharp pole in his gloved hand, twisted round in the saddle and faced them. Max found himself staring at a metal visor with a single narrow slit. Max couldn't see the eyes behind it but a lump of fear came to his throat. Whoever the eyes belonged to could see him quite clearly and was looking directly at him.

Chapter Eight

Max sat on the ground where he'd fallen, and kept very still. Walking around in this world of stories was like being in an exceptionally frightening computer game. You never knew what was going to pop out at you. His heart hammered in his chest as he stared at the knight.

"Watch where you're going, will you?" The horse and its rider towered over Nettle but she stood right in front of them with her hands on her hips – very unwisely, in Max's opinion.

The knight raised his gloved hand and Max winced, convinced he was going to reach down and strike Nettle a fatal blow.

Instead, the knight lifted his visor.

"A thousand pardons, fair damsel!" he said, revealing a

pair of bright blue eyes and a very bushy moustache which spilled out of the helmet. "Do excuse my excessive blunder. I didn't realise there was anybody here." He turned to Max. "No bones broken, I trust, young squire?"

Max shook his head. Now that he could see his face, the knight didn't look too bad. His booming voice sounded friendly too.

"Good, good," the knight chortled. "Now if all's well, time's a-wasting and I have fish to fry! I'm in pursuit, don't ye know! Onward, Nobility, my trusty steed!"

"No, wait!" Nettle cried. "Have you seen a witch go by, with a little—"

But the knight was already pointing his horse and his lance in the direction he had been heading.

Then he stopped.

"Oh, flog it! It's gone!"

"What's gone?" Max craned his head but he couldn't see anything other than fields and hedges.

"Wretched rainbow, squire," said the knight. "Didn't you see it? It was up that way, in the west. Darned elusive things, rainbows. Been tilting at 'em all my days and never caught one yet." He twirled a length of sandy moustache. "Got pretty close once or twice, mind ye. 'Tis only a matter of time."

"I thought knights were supposed to chase dragons and things, not rainbows," Nettle said.

"You're not alone in that style of thinking, young madam," said the knight, clanking a leg up and over and sliding down from his horse. "Many's the time I've been advised I'm on a hiding to naught, frittering my life away. 'Give it a rest, Sir Gladalad,' folk used to say. 'You're never going to cover yourself in glory that way. Do something useful instead.'"

"Sir . . . Gladalad?" Nettle said.

"That's me," said the knight. "Should have said before. Been so long since I've seen a body or a soul, I've forgotten how to behave. Etiquette, and all that – gone rusty, just like my armour!" He laughed and bowed as low as his creaking armour would allow, wheeling his hand round in circles as he did so. "Sir Gladalad Gadabout, at your service. How do ye do?"

At your service. Max liked the sound of those words. This knight didn't seem to be afraid, like the people he'd met at Happy End. *He* wasn't hiding away in the palace. A fearless knight was just what they needed.

"Hello," he said, standing and brushing grass from the turn-ups of his short trousers. "I'm Max."

"Greetings, Max. Sorry we up-ended you. Spot of knickerbocker trouble there, I see." The knight guffawed, then gazed off into the distance. He still seemed disappointed about the rainbow.

"I wonder if you could help us," Max said, as politely as possible. "You see, we're on a quest."

"Ah ha," said Sir Gladalad, reluctantly tearing his eyes away from the sky. He smiled in a way that made his already curly moustache curl a little more. "A quest, is it? Splendid. Wondered what brought you. I haven't seen anyone on these plains for many a month."

"How long have you been here?" Max asked.

"Thirty-seven moons, maybe longer."

Max did a quick calculation in his head. That was over three years. He firmly hoped they weren't going to be here for that long. Anyway, they couldn't be. They only had two days.

"Why have you been out here so long?" Nettle asked, patting the broad nose of Sir Gladalad's huge horse. "Are you lost?"

"Not lost, dear girl. Banished. Got banished, ye see, in the Long Summer of Yore."

"Who by?" Nettle asked.

"What for?" Max added. That was more to the point. A knight in armour might be helpful on the quest – but not if he was a criminal.

"Banished by a lord, as a matter of fact," Sir Gladalad said, a little sheepishly. "'Twas Lord Malberry."

"We've heard of him." Nettle gave Max a meaningful look.

"Yes? Not surprised. Powerful fella. He got fed up with me, all right. 'Tis the rainbow-chasing, don't ye know.

83

Got to be a bit of a habit. I was to marry Lord Malberry's daughter, the fair Lady Willamina, but I kept dashing after the rainbows and he claimed I wasn't good enough for her. Said I had to live alone out here in the wilderness until I came to my senses. I wasn't to show my face at Happy End until I'd proved I had true . . . true . . . now, what was it?" He scratched the top of his helmet. "Ah yes, I remember. True mettle."

"What's true mettle?" Max asked. If Sir Gladalad had it, whatever it was, it could be useful to them on the quest.

"Not entirely sure. That's half the problem, old squire. But I imagine I haven't shown it yet, since I'm still here!" Sir Gladalad gave a rueful chuckle.

"What about Lady Willamina?" Nettle said.

"Good question. Spirited girl, she is. Got terrifically angry and told Lord Malberry it was none of his business who she married."

"Good for her!" said Nettle.

"Quite so," said Sir Gladalad. "Trouble was, old Malberry didn't like it – always hated being defied. Used a drop of magic on her, I shouldn't wonder. Don't know what he transformed her into. A swan, most likely. I see a flock of 'em flying over here from time to time. I always call her name but no swan ever answers. Nor even turns its lovely long neck in my direction. Willamina had a neck, I can tell you, white and soft as snow." He sniffed. "Snappy dresser too, all her own style. Liked to wear men's trews. Practical, you see, not like the other damsels."

"And now you're apart all the time. That's so sad," Nettle said, staring up at the sky.

Max guessed she was thinking about Wild and how she was apart from him, too. It was terrible to imagine him all alone with that dreadful witch.

"Holdy hard!" Sir Gladalad bellowed suddenly. "There's one of 'em now!"

"A swan?" Max scanned the sky.

"No, lad. A rainbow!" With a clunk of metal Sir Gladalad straddled his horse. "Lovely chatting and consorting with you both, but I must away."

"Wait!" Nettle said. "You can't just leave us. My little brother's missing!"

"That's right," said Max. "Babs Haggard has stolen him. We think she's taken him to Beyond. We're on our way to find him."

Sir Gladalad tucked the ends of his moustache away in his helmet. "Dashed sorry to hear that. But I don't recommend a trip to Beyond. 'Tis a terrible place by all accounts. No one's ever come back from there. And you don't want to go climbing Harsh Mountain. Far too treacherous." He gathered the horse's reins as it staggered sideways, eager to be off on the chase. "No. Best you two green saplings turn around and go back to the safety of wherever 'tis you've come from."

"No!" A wave of nausea had rolled over Max at the mention of Harsh Mountain, but he rushed forward, determined to stop Sir Gladalad from leaving. The presence of an adult was reassuring, even if that adult was an exceedingly flaky knight from some ancient made-up story. If he could just make him understand the seriousness of the situation, he might stay with them.

"We can't go back," he said. "We're on a quest to defeat Babs Haggard, you see. We think she's killed Lord Malberry."

"What's that?" Sir Gladalad looked startled. "Malberry's dead, you say?"

"Yes. And she's going to kill all the happy endings too. She's taking over the whole of your world with her evil."

"Taking over Ever After?"

"Yes. You're so keen on rainbows you probably haven't noticed. But can't you see how cold and grey everything's turning? Haven't you felt the fierce winds?"

"Can't say I have." The knight looked around. "Though now you come to mention it, there have been some devilish nasty mists floating in of late, clouding up the rainbows, et cetera . . ."

"You have to help us," Max insisted. "If we don't stop Babs Haggard, there won't be any more happy endings ever again. Not for you or anyone else!" And, he thought to himself, he and Nettle and Wild would never get home.

The knight seemed to hesitate, his eyes flickering between the two of them and the distant rainbow.

"Please come," Max said, racking his brains for something more persuasive.

"Yes, please do," Nettle said, adding, "you never know, we might even find your Lady Willamina on the way."

Max had to admit that was brilliant. It was the something extra he had been searching for. Sir Gladalad clearly loved this Lady Willamina. Surely he'd come with them now.

"Love to accompany you," Sir Gladalad said. "Nothing I'd like more. Trouble is," he turned away from them, "Trouble is, I'm a hopeless case . . ." He clicked his tongue. "Onward, Nobility. A rainbow calls!"

"Please stop!" Nettle called as he cantered away.

"What about us?" Max shouted. He couldn't believe Sir Gladalad was deserting them. "At least tell us how long it will take us to get there."

"By all means," Sir Gladalad hollered back. "If you go at a fair lick you'll be off the plains and over the two valleys in a few hours. You should be at Harsh Mountain by nightfall."

"Have you heard of the Shining Pathway?" Nettle called. "Do you know anything about that?"

But the knight only saluted as he rode. "Fare ye well, young adventurers! Rainbow ho!" He dropped his visor and broke into a gallop. "Rainbow hooooooo!"

They stood listening to the last echoes of Sir Gladalad's voice, and the fading clip clop of his horse's hooves.

Nettle stamped her foot.

"So much for blimmin' knights in blimmin' shining armour!"

"I know." Max nodded. "Not that his armour *was* very shiny." Sir Gladalad hadn't behaved like a gallant knight at all; he hadn't shown any interest in helping to rescue Wild. "What story is Sir Gladalad Gadabout from anyway?"

Nettle shrugged. "Not one I know."

So she didn't know all the stories after all. Max considered saying so but it didn't seem fair. Especially since she'd pushed him out of the way of Sir Gladalad's horse, saving his life for the second time that day. And anyway, he'd had enough of arguing.

"So," he said. "What now?" Although he already knew the answer.

"We keep going, of course. To Harsh Mountain." Nettle pulled her leafy jacket around her. She began walking, and Max followed.

The closer they came to the mountain, the bigger and more unconquerable it seemed. Max generally avoided risky activities of all kinds, but climbing was his absolute worst. Mum had been a brilliant climber. It was sort of her job. She was like Spiderman. She never fell off anything or even lost her footing, except that one last time when the avalanche came. Even Mum couldn't do anything about that. Max had never had a head for heights himself, but now heights were the things he hated most in all the world.

Every bit of him wanted to turn round and flee for his life, but he kept walking. Walking and walking towards Harsh Mountain, the highest height he'd ever seen in his life. How could a boy like him, he thought for the hundredth time, a boy who was terrified of heights and pretty much everything else, possibly be the one to save the Land of Ever After?

✤ Chapter Nine ✤

"How much further?" Max wondered aloud. "We must have walked for miles."

They had been trudging over the fields, their eyes fixed on Harsh Mountain, for hours, but they didn't seem to be getting any closer. The sickly, pale sun was going steadily downwards and a cold wind blew into their faces. A thick grey mist had gathered low around their ankles so that Max couldn't even see his aching feet. He hopped along behind Nettle, trying to brush grit off the soles of his slippers. He didn't need to look at them to know they were completely worn through. His feet were killing him.

"I've never walked this far before. Not even when we did orienteering at school." At least he'd had boots then and a proper coat. "Can you see any sign of the Shining Path?"

Nettle didn't answer. She seemed to be saving all her energy for walking, ploughing grimly on ahead of him. He wouldn't have minded if she'd talked to him a bit. Even her rudeness would have been better than listening to the anxious cries he could hear in the distance. He couldn't see anyone, they were too far off, but he could tell they were people in a hurry. The words *escape*, *safety* and *Happy End* carried their way to him on the wind, being repeated over and over. He wondered just how safe Happy End really was. The palace hadn't seemed too secure when he was there; it could be even less so by now. He shuddered as he remembered the moan that had come from the giant's mouth, and the twitching of his enormous fingers. Whoever these people were, he hoped they made it to Happy End alive. And he hoped it would be Bill Fairfoul who greeted them there, not some terrifying giant.

Talking would have distracted him from worrying about Dad too. What would Dad have done when they didn't appear out of the cake? What was he doing now? Was he already sitting with some police officer, shoulders slumped, preparing to go on national television and make an appeal for Max to come home? Was he crying? Just thinking about it made Max want to cry himself.

And he was hungry. It was odd to be thinking about food at a time like this but the wedding lunch, which they'd missed, must have been over ages ago and his stomach was grumbling like mad. So was Nettle's. He could hear it gurgle as she marched ahead of him. They'd passed a solitary apple tree full of red and green fruit, but as soon as they'd picked an apple and bitten into it, its skin had turned grey, and its flesh pulpy and rotten. Babs Haggard's grip on Ever After seemed to be tightening by the minute.

"What's school like?" Nettle said suddenly, still walking in front of him.

That was an odd question. "What? What do you mean?"

"I mean, what's it like?" Nettle tossed her head impatiently. At least she was talking to him.

"Don't you know?"

"No. I've never been to school. Ilona home-schools me so we can go travelling. I've been to eleven different countries. And Wild's been to five."

"Really? I never knew that."

"Don't know much about us, do you?"

It was true. He hardly knew anything about Nettle and Wild. He hadn't wanted to know. Whenever Dad had tried talking to him about Ilona and her family, Max had switched off and slipped away as quickly as possible to work on his marble run.

"Do you like travelling, then?" Going to faraway countries wasn't Max's idea of fun. He liked being at home where he knew the routine and exactly what dinner would taste like.

"I love it. I love going to new places. We're not doing

it any more though, now that Ilona's marrying your dad. We're settling down. Worse luck." Nettle pulled a leaf off her jacket, scrunched it between her fingers and let it fall.

"I see."

Max wasn't happy about the wedding but it had never occurred to him that Nettle might not be too pleased about it either. He'd never tried to look at it from her point of view. Perhaps he should have done.

"Why do you call her Ilona? She is your mum, isn't she?"

"Of course." Nettle shrugged. "Ilona doesn't like labels. She's a free spirit. Me and Wild are free spirits too." Max couldn't think of an answer to that. He noticed that the mist was rising, circling their waists and becoming more dense. He couldn't see his hands now unless he lifted them out of the mist.

"So what's it like?" Nettle said again. "Do you have a uniform and school dinners and stuff?"

"Oh yes, all of that," he said, pleased to be asked to think about something ordinary for once. "School's OK, I suppose. My teacher's Mr Burton. He's quite good, but he's a bit strict. Tony and Rio once put their chewed chewing gum on his chair and he sat on it and it stuck to his trousers. He was so angry, he went purple! It was really funny."

"Tony and Rio are idiots," Nettle announced.

"You don't know," Max retorted. "You've never met them."

"It's obvious. There's nothing funny about ruining someone's trousers."

Nettle was so quick to react and so certain about everything. If they'd been in Mansley and not in this serious situation, Max might have told her to stop being such a know-all. Although now he came to think about it, the chewing gum incident hadn't been all that funny. And he'd never seen Mr Burton in those trousers since. All the same, if anyone was going to say Tony and Rio were idiots, it ought to be him, not Nettle.

Nettle stopped suddenly and Max bumped into her.

"I've lost it!"

"Lost what? What's wrong?"

"The path we were on. I can't see it any more."

Max watched the mist spread out in front of them like deep water. It was very disconcerting not being able to see where they were putting their feet, but surely all they had to do was keep walking towards the mountain? He was about to say so when he saw that just a little further on, the mist ramped up into the sky like a steep ski slope. Harsh Mountain was no longer visible. Not even the top.

The two of them turned slowly round on the spot. Long heavy curtains of mist hung all around them. When they stopped turning, Max realised he no longer knew which way he was facing. Towards Harsh Mountain and Beyond, or back the way they had come.

"Which way is it? Which way?" Nettle kicked angrily at the mist. "The witch must be doing this. She must know we're on our way. She's trying to stop us!"

"Or else it's a trap." Max swallowed nervously.

He lifted his marble net so he could see it and passed it anxiously from hand to hand. If Babs Haggard attacked them here, they would have no chance. He wished he could go back in time to when he'd woken up that morning. He'd refuse to get out of bed. He'd stay there for the whole day and then none of this could happen.

Something moved very close by in the scrubby grass. Max yelped and instinctively grabbed Nettle's arm.

"What was that?"

"What?" She pushed his hand away. "I didn't see anything."

"There's something out there."

He froze, listening intently. First there was nothing, but then he heard the swish of grass. His eyes followed the sound and he saw the silhouette of a boy, darting through the fog.

"Can't catch me!"

The mist cleared a little and Max recognised the short boy he'd glimpsed before. He still had his arms in the air but he didn't look quite so brown now. He had grey patches on him, and he wasn't running quite so fast.

"Wait!" Nettle shouted, seeing him too.

"Run, run as fast as you can," the boy called over his

shoulder in a tiny, rasping voice. "You can't catch me."

"Hold on a minute!" Nettle said. "Isn't that . . . ?"

"I'm the gingerbread man!" The boy leaped high, curled into a ball and somersaulted up into the air and away from them. He landed, ran on and disappeared into the mist.

"The gingerbread man!" Nettle exclaimed. "That is so weird."

Of course it was the gingerbread man. Max should have realised. That was why he had his arms stuck in the air all the time – he'd been made with a biscuit cutter.

"I saw him before," he said. "I wish he'd just stand still for a moment. He might know something about the Shining Pathway. We could have asked him for directions."

"At least he's made a path," Nettle said. She was right. The gingerbread man's somersaulting body had hollowed out a sort of tunnel in the mist. "Although it's not exactly shiny."

"Should we follow it, do you think?" Max gazed around. He didn't know if it was the right way or not, but it was the only way there was.

"We'll have to," Nettle said.

They walked, stooping, into the tunnel of mist. Max couldn't see an end to the tunnel and it felt claustrophobic, much worse than being inside the cake. He hoped it wasn't going to bring on a panic attack.

"Your mum gave you those marbles, didn't she?"

Until Nettle spoke, Max hadn't even realised he was still

holding his marble net. Hastily he put it away in his pocket.

"How did you know?"

"She died three years ago. Ilona told me that. You've had the marbles for three years and never opened them. You get really stressy if anyone touches them. It's obvious."

"What are you, some kind of detective?" Max couldn't help being impressed at how quickly Nettle worked things out but he didn't like anyone knowing how important the marbles were to him. If Tony and Rio found out, they might not understand. They'd say he was a baby.

"Don't tell anyone about them, will you? If we get home, I mean?" None of it would matter at all if they never got back to Mansley.

"Like who? Who would I tell? Wild?"

"No, I don't mind about him." Wild was only little. Max couldn't imagine Wild ever being mean or teasing him about anything.

"I'm not telling those losers at your school, if that's what you're thinking," Nettle said. "If I do start there in September I won't be telling those two anything."

"You're going to my school?" This was news to Max. He'd known for a while that he was going to have to share a house with Nettle. He hadn't imagined he would have to see her all day at school too. Had Dad told him about this? Had he just not been listening?

"Do you want to go?" he asked. He wasn't worried about

97

Tony and Rio making his life a misery now. If she chose to, Nettle could do that all by herself.

"Maybe. Maybe not. Wild wants to go. He can't wait to start school. And I wouldn't mind knowing what it's like, being in a proper classroom all day, learning loads of different stuff."

The ground they were walking on was rough and Max winced at every step. He tried to take his mind off his feet by imagining Nettle at school. He'd have to introduce her, probably, on the first day of term. What would everyone else make of her? She wasn't like the other girls he knew. He bet the girls would be quite impressed by her, though, even if Tony and Rio weren't.

"Hurry up, Max," she said now. "What do you keep stopping for? Something wrong with your feet?"

"Yes. I've got blisters, thanks to these stupid shoes Ilona made me wear." He glanced at Nettle, remembering it was her mother he was talking about. "No offence," he added.

Nettle smirked. "It's OK. I didn't want to wear this stupid leaf suit either."

"Really?" Max had always thought of Ilona and Nettle and Wild as a sort of package. They were one type of person and he was another. He hadn't considered that Nettle might not like all the same things her mother liked.

"Why did you go along with it then?"

"Because she seemed so happy. I didn't want to burst her bubble. She really likes your dad."

"He really likes her too," Max said. "But I guess we knew that."

"Yes," Nettle agreed. "Guess we did."

It occurred to Max that in many ways he and Nettle were in the same boat. They were both being forced to give up a way of life that suited them because of their parents' marriage. Maybe that was why she treated him so badly. Thinking about it, he probably hadn't treated her too well either. Maybe he should have made a bit more effort.

They walked silently for a while, the mist coiling around them, and then Nettle said, "I'm sorry about your mum dying and everything."

"Oh. Thanks."

It was odd, Nettle coming right out and mentioning Mum like that.

"It must have been really horrible for you."

"Yeah," Max said. "It was."

No one at school ever talked about Mum, or the fact that he didn't have one any longer. They were too embarrassed. He felt a bit embarrassed himself right now but he tried not to show it because at least Nettle had started to be a bit nicer to him.

He wondered what he could say to be nice back. Maybe something about Ilona. He thought she was quite pretty.

He could say something about her clothes. The tassels and fringey bits on her dresses. All those scarves that kept getting caught on door handles. That probably wasn't quite the right thing. Before he could think what was the right thing, they came out of the tunnel of mist and found themselves back out in the open.

They were at the far edge of the wide plain. They had crossed it successfully. The two valleys Sir Gladalad had mentioned lay ahead, the only things left between them and Harsh Mountain. The mountain was clearly visible again now and it looked much, much closer. Its sharp shadow loomed right over the valleys and seemed to point directly at them.

Max took a deep breath. It wouldn't be long now before they met their fate, whatever it was to be. Falling from a mountain, being killed by Babs Haggard, or perhaps turned to stone for all eternity. Whatever it was, it would all be over soon. He reckoned it would only take them another hour or so to walk to the mountain. The sun was low but it ought to be light long enough. He was about to say so when Nettle ran forward.

"Hello! What are *you* doing here?" she exclaimed.

She sounded so excited that for a moment Max thought she'd seen Wild, but when he looked over there were three long-haired kittens, trotting to meet her. They gathered round her, rubbing their pretty heads against her knees.

"Look, Max, they're so cute!" She crouched down and tickled them under their chins, laughing as one of them licked her wrist. "Oh dear, are you hungry? I'm sorry we haven't got any food for you. Where did you three come from? Are you from the nursery rhyme? Are you the three little kittens who lost their mittens?"

The kittens did look adorable. They were so soft and sweet-looking, so unlike the harsh landscape they'd just crossed. Max felt like stroking them too, but something made him stay back. What were three such well-groomed kittens doing out here all alone on the plain? Had someone left them behind, maybe, in their haste to get to Happy End? It didn't quite add up.

"Nettle. Don't. We've got to keep going, remember? Hold on, we don't know if they're—"

Before he could go on, the licking kitten's tongue suddenly grew, stretching out of its mouth until it was as long as Max's school tie.

"Watch out!" Max cried.

"Oh!" Nettle recoiled, but it was already too late. The disgusting tongue had wrapped itself firmly round her wrist while, to Max's horror, the rest of the kitten began to bulge and grow.

As he watched, the other kittens grew too. Their mews and purrs turned to fierce hisses and menacing growls. In a matter of seconds there was no longer any sign of the cute little kittens. Instead, Max found himself staring at three huge wild cats, all of them surrounding Nettle.

And it wasn't food they were interested in. It was Nettle herself.

Chapter Ten

Max stared in shock as the cat with the long tongue seized Nettle's elbow in its teeth. A second cat took hold of her other elbow and she gasped with pain. The third cat stood on its hind legs and grabbed her hair, then dropped to all fours, dragging Nettle down with it. They pinned her to the ground.

"Max!"

"Nettle!"

Max took a step forward, but as soon as he did so, the cats whipped their heads in his direction, snarling, daring him to come nearer.

He stopped, his feet glued to the ground. He was about as mobile as his bedroom cupboard. He was so scared. All he could do was watch Nettle struggle.

Then the animals began to drag her away.

"Max!" she yelled. "Do something! Please!"

It flashed through Max's mind that if Nettle was taken away now he would have to continue the quest on his own. It would be a hundred times worse then.

He forced himself on a few steps and stopped again. What could he do? He needed a weapon. He remembered the brooch that held his cape, and undid it. He moved forward tentatively, holding the brooch pin out in front of him. Maybe he could stab one of the cats with it. But even if he dared, he'd never get near enough to manage it. The pin was only about four centimetres long. He stood still again, stuck.

"Get help!" Nettle shouted.

"Where from?" Even if he'd had a phone he couldn't exactly call the emergency services. He glanced around wildly. Nothing. Just trees, bushes, the sky and a rainbow.

A rainbow! Had Sir Gladalad seen it? If the knight was nearby he might still be able to help. Surely he would help them now, if he saw what terrible trouble Nettle was in. Or if he wouldn't, Max could at least borrow his sword or his lance. Even he might be able to whack the cats on the head if he was on the other end of a long lance.

Max cupped his hands to his mouth and yelled, "Rainbow!"

The wild cats pricked their ears, but continued to pull Nettle away.

"Rainbow! Rainbow!" Max screamed. Nothing happened. Nettle had begged him to help her and all he was doing was standing still and shouting about rainbows. Some hero he was. He sounded like a hysterical idiot, but he kept shouting. "Rainbow!"

"Rainbow hooooooooo!" Max felt a rush of relief as a deep answering cry reached him and a horse came powering out of the mist.

"I hear you, lad," Sir Gladalad Gadabout called jovially, galloping into view. "Caught the rainbow bug, have ye? Glad to hear it. Care to join me in a tilt?"

He was so busy looking at the rainbow that he didn't notice Nettle being dragged away, scudding across the ground. How could he possibly not see her?

"No!" Max shouted, surprised at the strength of his own voice. "That's not it at all. You have to rescue Nettle! Look! She's there! She's being abducted by wild cats!"

"What's that you say?" Sir Gladalad cupped a hand to his ear, but there was no stopping him. He drove Nobility on full pelt towards the spot where Nettle was lying.

Max screamed. Nettle wasn't going to be torn apart by wild cats after all. She was going to be trampled by a huge horse. And it would all be his fault.

He was hardly able to look as the horse suddenly took

off into the air. It flew right over Nettle, its great hooves kicking, sending the wild cats flying in all directions.

Max sighed with relief. At least Nobility was looking where he was going.

"Clattering clobberjays!" Sir Gladalad exclaimed, finally noticing Nettle, as he and Nobility landed, a safe distance from her head. "That don't look like a joy ride, young maiden. That don't look comfy. Where'd that pack of angry felines spring from?"

The three battered cats got up and limped towards one another. They gathered together, heads touching. And suddenly they weren't wild cats any longer. They were chicken feet. Bloodied and bruised, yellow chicken feet. They were Babs Haggard's agents!

The chicken feet could turn into anything, it seemed. Sugary mice, cuddly kittens or fearsome beasts. Max felt sure their presence could only mean one thing. Babs Haggard knew Wild wasn't in Ever After alone. She knew they were there too, on their way to Beyond, and she had sent out her agents to cut them off. He wished they'd been more cautious. After all, Bill Fairfoul had warned them. What if Babs Haggard herself appeared now too, as she had before?

But she didn't. And without her to command them, the chicken feet seemed confused. They scratched uncertainly at the ground with their talons.

Max picked up a stone and threw it at them. He grabbed another and threw that too.

"Get lost!" he shouted. "Get out of here!"

"Yes, quite right." Sir Gladalad waved a gauntlet. "Do as the young squire says. Be off with you! Shoo! Shoo!"

The chicken feet staggered around drunkenly, then careered away. They scuttled into the air, and with three sharp popping sounds, they vanished.

Max stared in amazement. "Where did they go?"

"Back to base, I imagine," said Sir Gladalad. "Lost this skirmish and been recalled to regroup."

Max shuddered, realising that he hadn't seen the last of the hideous chicken feet. At least they had gone for now. Once he was sure of that, he ran over to where Nettle was lying.

"Are you all right?"

"I don't know. My arm hurts." She clutched her arm, which seemed to be sticking out at an odd angle. She looked pale, sick with pain. How could she go any further like that? Max worried.

"Dislocated shoulder, for sure," said Sir Gladalad. "Can spot 'em a mile off."

Leaping down from Nobility, he clanked over to Nettle. "May I?" He plucked off his gauntlets. Nettle looked at him uncertainly as he took hold of her arm.

"Splendid. Now all you have to do is say, 'One, two and a bucket of true.'"

"Is that some sort of healing spell?" Max said. "What are you going to do to her?" Sir Gladalad didn't look much like a doctor. He might make things even worse.

"Off you go, now." Sir Gladalad waited, with his eyes shut, holding Nettle's arm in his two hands. "Soon as you like."

"One, two . . ." Nettle began weakly, "and a bucket of . . . Aaaagh!" She cried out in pain as the knight suddenly pulled, bent and pushed at her arm.

"Home again!" he announced, letting go.

Nettle touched her shoulder and moved her arm experimentally. "It's better!"

"Knew it would be." Sir Gladalad put his gauntlets back on. "Nothing to it! My Lady Willamina taught me that little trick. Darned useful, as it turns out."

To Max's amazement the knight leaped back onto his waiting horse.

"Where are you going now?"

"Why, on with the rainbow hunt, of course. Sure you wouldn't care to accompany me, lad? Not too late to change your mind." He patted the saddle behind him as if he expected Max to leap up and join him.

Max jumped up and down in frustration.

"How can you think about rainbows at a time like this?"

Nettle could have died just then. Why couldn't the knight see? Babs Haggard was on to them. She knew they were close so she'd sent her chicken feet to catch them. She was trying to pick them off, one by one. First Nettle, and then him.

He grabbed hold of the spur that stuck out of Sir Gladalad's armoured boot. "You can't leave us on our own now. You have to help!"

"But, my rainbow . . ." Sir Gladalad protested. He sounded like a little boy.

"Forget the rainbows," Max said. The knight was so annoying. "Rainbows aren't real. You can't actually catch up with them or get to the ends of them. Rainbows are nothing, just optical illusions. They're a trick of the light!"

"Really?" The knight seemed disappointed. "Dashed shame, if so." He gazed at the rainbow curved over the distant hills and sighed. "What beautiful trickery, though."

"And another thing," Max went on, desperately trying to get through to the man. "If Babs Haggard gets her way, it won't just be the happy endings that she ruins. It will be *everything* that's beautiful – the whole of Ever After, even the sun. And that'll be the end of your stupid rainbows!"

"Egad!" Sir Gladalad exclaimed, swinging round in his saddle. "That's grave news indeed, lad. In that case, there's no time to lose."

And just as Max thought he'd seen sense and would agree

to help them at last, Sir Gladalad clicked his tongue. "Come on, Nobility, my fiery steed. This could be our last chance, confound it! We'd better make the most of it!" He readied his lance and cantered away in the direction of the already-fading rainbow.

"You stupid, stupid fool!" Max yelled after him.

"Leave him," Nettle said. It was a relief to see her sitting up. "There's no point. He's an idiot, a poor lost soul. Bill Fairfoul said we should keep an eye out for them, remember."

"But why?" Max protested, going over and helping her to her feet. "What's the point of them if they aren't going to be any use to us?" Her arm looked straight enough but her face had a greenish tinge, as if she might be sick. "Can you walk, do you think?"

"I don't know." Shakily Nettle looked up at the dim sun. Only half of it was showing now, beyond the hills. "But we need to get moving. We can't leave Wild with that witch for a whole night."

"I know," Max said. They really needed to get to the mountain by nightfall, although he knew that even if they found a way to climb it, it would be impossible to get over it in darkness. No one climbed at night. He couldn't face telling Nettle that, though. Not yet.

Together, they started to stride away, but then Nettle sank down.

Max tried to help her up.

"What is it? Have you got more injuries?" The wild-cat chicken legs must have damaged more than just her shoulder.

Nettle shook her head. "No. I just feel wobbly. Sort of faint."

Max wished he had some food to offer Nettle, but there was nothing in his pockets, just Wild's crayon, his marbles and Tilly's juniper berries, which Nettle had told him were basically inedible. If only he hadn't given the hotel sweets to the troll, they could have eaten those. Perhaps he should have given her the marbles after all, but he knew he could never part with them, not for anyone or anything.

"Wild," Nettle said, struggling to stand. "We have to get to Wild. We have to find the Shining Pathway!"

"OK, we're going." Whatever else, they had to keep moving. If they stayed where they were he was afraid it would only be a matter of time before the chicken feet returned in some new, horrible disguise. He would have to help Nettle along.

Gingerly, he put an arm round her waist. He half expected her to push him off, but she didn't. She put her arm round his shoulders so that he could support her better.

"Off we go, then." He tried to sound positive as they made for the trees, and he tried to ignore his ragged slippers and blistered feet. They hobbled along awkwardly and, although Max was still very scared, he at least felt as if he was playing a part now. He was helping Nettle, and she was letting him.

111

They might not be friends but they weren't exactly enemies either. They had a job to do together and they were trying to do it. Although, if anyone could see them stumbling along now, Max thought, they wouldn't look like conquering heroes, but more like a pair of losers in a three-legged race.

Chapter Eleven

Lots of people saw them, or would have done, if any of them had had space in their minds to give two ragged strangers even a split second's thought. The plains had been deserted apart from Sir Gladalad and the witch's horrible chicken feet, but there were villages in the two valleys, full of creatures and characters, all of them packing up and running for their lives.

The first sign of life was a bird, a swallow, spinning and diving like an out-of-control plane. It whizzed between their heads, close enough for Max to catch the look of terror on the face of its tiny passenger.

"Thumbelina!" Nettle breathed, but the miniature girl didn't even turn her head, just clung grimly to the swallow's tail feathers, from which she looked set to fall at any moment.

"Swallow can't fly properly," she cried. "He's been sabotaged!"

"Who by?" Max called. Thumbelina was concentrating so hard on holding on that she didn't reply, though Max was pretty sure he already knew the answer.

No sooner had Thumbelina passed than the sky was lit up with a flash of lightning and they were almost knocked down by three pigs hurtling towards them.

"Fire! Fire! Fire!" they squealed. "It came from nowhere! It was spontaneous combustion!"

Their hooves skittered on the ground as they stumbled past, clutching what Max guessed must be their most treasured possessions: a clock, a portrait of an elderly pig with hairy ears, and a reddish hen, terror shining in her beady eye.

The air smelled strongly of smoke and it wasn't long before Max and Nettle came to a house of bricks, half burned to the ground, long past saving. Orange daggers of flame pointed high above it and waved, almost triumphantly, into the darkening sky.

"I thought they were safe in the brick house," Max said, remembering the story of the Three Little Pigs.

"They were," Nettle answered, a grim expression on her face. "Safe from the wolf, anyway."

Even a house of bricks, Max thought with a shudder, was no protection against Babs Haggard's magic. It was just as

Bill Fairfoul had feared. As she gained in power, the witch was meddling in every story, ruining the ending of each one.

As if to confirm that fact, thunder rumbled overhead like evil, throaty laughter. Long cracks of lightning split the sky.

Max and Nettle put their heads down and kept going. They passed other houses, huts and dwelling places, either abandoned already or in the process of being so. Around them, girls and boys, winged fairies and elves, and old men and women milled about, salvaging things from their homes, then rushing away in panic.

Nettle kept trying to stop people and ask about the Shining Pathway; Max did too, but everyone sidestepped or shouldered past them, either too busy or too scared to pause for a single moment. And no wonder, thought Max. Because every now and again there was a popping sound, like a crisp packet bursting, and one of the escaping crowd would be turned into a toad. The poor creatures were left hopping in circles, croaking rustily, as people dodged them, screaming and running even faster to avoid the same fate.

Max flinched at every thunder clap. Everyone was rushing in the opposite direction to the one he and Nettle were heading in. If she hadn't been leaning on him, he thought he might have turned tail and joined the stampede himself because the closer they got to Harsh Mountain, the more terrible things were becoming. But he knew this was the way he had to go if he was ever to get back to Dad. And there was

Wild, of course. *He* hadn't had a chance to run away. He was depending on them. Max didn't know what Babs Haggard meant to do to Wild but whatever it was, he and Nettle needed to get to Beyond before she did it.

Trudging out of the first of the two valleys, Max glanced up at the towering mountain that stood between them and the witch's domain. Their only hope of getting over it was to find the Shining Pathway that Bill Fairfoul had told them about. Maybe, if it was magic in some way, it could help them; but as far as he could see, there was nothing that resembled a path on the black surface of the rock face, or anything even remotely shiny. He was beginning to wonder if the Shining Pathway even existed.

He was just wishing he'd tried to stop someone and ask them when he caught sight of a black-haired boy. His head was twisted awkwardly away from them and he was limping along, lagging behind the escaping crowds. Max found he was beginning to remember more of his old stories now and he immediately thought of the boy in the Pied Piper, the lame one who hadn't been able to keep up with the other children. Maybe this was him. Maybe he knew something that would help them.

"Hey!" he called. "Do you know anything about the Shining Pathway?"

"Never heard of it!" the boy shouted at once. Then he yelped as if he'd just been bitten.

"Are you sure?" Nettle said. "It should be somewhere on the mountain. Please think carefully. It's very important."

"There's no such thing as the Shining Pathway! Ow!" The boy cried out again.

"That's not true. You're lying!" Nettle said fiercely. She knew as well as Max that the Shining Pathway was their only chance of getting to Wild.

"I never lie! Ai! Ai! Ow!"

The boy turned towards them then and Max saw, with a shock, why he was limping and crying out so much. His nose was as thick and as long as an elephant's trunk and it dragged along the ground as the boy walked.

"You're Pinocchio!" Max said.

"No I am not!" The nose extended further along the ground and the boy stumbled over it.

The boy was lying. He was definitely Pinocchio. His nose was getting longer with every lie he told. But, unlike Pinocchio in the story, he didn't seem at all happy about his lies. Max remembered Pinocchio being full of mischief and telling lies gleefully, but this boy looked miserable and his eyes were watering, with tears or pain. Both, probably.

"Please don't lie. We really need to know!" Nettle said. "The future of Ever After depends on it! Don't you care about saving your world?"

"I don't care about it. Not one little itty bit!" the boy said, and his nose grew even longer.

117

Max felt Nettle stiffen next to him. "And what if I told you Babs Haggard was holding my baby brother hostage?" she shouted at the boy. "What would you say then?"

"Couldn't care less!"

"Then . . . then your heart must be hard and wooden, just like the rest of you!"

Nettle looked as if she would like to rush over to the boy and kick him, like she'd kicked Max before. Max didn't know if she'd have the strength to do something like that now but he took a firmer hold of her arm just in case. He could see the boy was sobbing as he tried to wrap the enormous nose around his waist so that he could carry it better. It wouldn't be fair to hurt him more than he was hurting already. It crossed Max's mind that every single thing this Pinocchio was saying was a lie and that he couldn't stop lying, even if he wanted to.

"Pay no attention," he said. "I don't think he can help it. I think Babs Haggard must have got to him already. She's put a spell on him."

"No she hasn't," the boy retorted. "That witch has got nothing to do with it. Babs Haggard is a very lovely person. She's never hurt anyone, or killed anyone or eaten anyone. She's really, really kind and generous, and she deserves to rule the world! And anyway, I like having a really long nose." From the wretched look on his face, Max could tell the boy didn't mean a single word he was saying.

"Leave him," he said, pulling Nettle onwards. "He doesn't know what he's talking about. Try and find Gepetto," he called after Pinocchio. "He might be able to help you."

"Don't care about Gepetto either," the boy said as he lurched away. "I don't care if I never see him again in my life! Ow! Don't care!"

The storm was subsiding now and Max and Nettle carried on, listening to the fading echoes of Pinocchio's cries. "Don't care! Ow! Don't care! Don't care!" Neither of them spoke until the echoes died out altogether.

"Well," Max said, breaking the silence and trying to sound optimistic, "at least if he was lying all the time we know that Pinocchio really has heard of the Shining Pathway."

"Yes," Nettle said, matching the brightness of his tone with hers. "That was good news, wasn't it? Now we can be sure it exists."

"And we're bound to find it soon."

"Bound to."

They were both doing their best to sound cheerful but Max knew they were both thinking about something else Pinocchio had said, about Babs Haggard.

She's never eaten anyone.

If Pinocchio said she hadn't eaten anyone, then that meant she had. Max had imagined Babs Haggard doing many things to Wild but he had never imagined for a moment that she might eat him. The prospect of it was too horrible to mention, let alone discuss. But he could tell Nettle was thinking about it too as she forced herself forward.

"We'll find it," she said and her lip trembled as she spoke. "We'll find the Shining Pathway."

She linked her arm in his. "We're almost there, aren't we, Max? So that's good news too, isn't it? We'll be up that mountain and in Beyond by nightfall." Sticking out her chin, she began to step up the pace. "Hold on, Wild," she said into the air ahead of her. "I'm on my way."

"Right," Max said huskily. He had to admire Nettle's bravery. If she wasn't going to crack and break down over this new danger to her brother, then he probably shouldn't either. He cleared his throat. "Good news. Right."

But with daylight fading and the temperature around them dropping like a stone, the prospect of reaching Beyond by nightfall, or any other time, certainly didn't feel like good news to Max.

Chapter Twelve

As they made their way out of the second valley, there were no more people or animals or any living creatures in sight. The last evidence of human existence they saw was a wishing well, belching out paper wishes which rained on their heads as they passed. They tried catching them but each time they did so, the words on the tiny papers vanished before they could read them and the wishes disintegrated. This was proof, Max thought, as a wish turned to ash in his hands, that one by one Babs Haggard was rubbing out the hopes of the entire story world.

The trees they walked among shuddered and dropped the last of their dead leaves on the ground. Neither Max nor Nettle mentioned that it had not been autumn but full summer when they had left Happy End earlier in the day.

Neither of them commented on the deep shadow that rolled over them once the weak sun had gone down, or the icy wind that nipped at their faces and numbed Max's toes.

Peering through the half-light, they left the naked, shivering trees behind and moved instead across rocky terrain, which soon became so thick with boulders it was difficult to pick a way through. And they didn't speak at all. Max figured Nettle was too exhausted now to spare any energy for talking, let alone arguing. And it was all he could do to keep them both upright. But mainly they were silent, Max knew, because they were thinking about Wild and what the witch meant to do to him.

Dusk had already turned to night when they finally reached the base of Harsh Mountain.

Max couldn't see the mountain any longer, but he could feel it. Its dark presence loomed above them and spread from side to side like a massive skirt, flowing out for miles. His hands met rock so hard and cold, it didn't seem possible that soft human hands could ever even have touched it before. It was an impossible obstacle. His legs began to tremble. His mum had been found at the bottom of a mountain just like this. His lovely, lively, strong and gentle mum. Grief surged like a cold river through his body and left him paralysed.

Next to him, Nettle laid her cheek on the unforgiving rock.

"Wild," she said.

She turned towards Max. "We've got to get over it, Max. We've got to!"

"We can't!" Max burst out. His legs weren't just shaking at the prospect of trying to climb this monster of a mountain; they were quaking with all the private bad feelings he'd been having since Mum died. It was like a bottle of concentrated pain had been unstoppered and poured all over him. "It's what I've been trying to tell you all – I'm the wrong person for the job. I hate mountains. I'm scared!"

Nettle was quiet. Then she said, "I know how your mum died. I know about the avalanche."

"Do you?" Max said gruffly. Of course she knew, everyone knew, but he didn't like her coming right out and saying it like that.

"Yes, your dad told me."

Dad had talked to Nettle, on his own, without Max. When had that happened?

"And he told me how brilliant she was too," Nettle added. "I bet you really loved her, didn't you?"

"There's no one like her," Max said. "No one in the world!" He hadn't meant to say that but his feelings were all so raw and at the very front of his mind, he couldn't help it. He screwed up his eyes and tried to remember Mum's face, but as always it was only a blur.

Nettle came closer. "Maybe *you're* like her. More than you realise. You're the son of a climber, Max, a fantastic climber. Maybe that's why you're here."

"It's not!" He smacked the rock with his hand. "It's all a mistake!" Nettle was just trying to make him feel better about himself, to persuade him to start climbing; but it was no good, she might as well stop right now. He hated mountains. He hated them. Mountains had taken Mum away from him forever. He never wanted to see another mountain as long as he lived. "It's too big a risk! Mum was brave, but I'm not!"

He rubbed his eyes. His face was soaking wet but he hadn't even known he was crying. He hoped Nettle hadn't noticed. She didn't say anything but he could feel her eyes on him in the dark.

"You saw me on that ladder," he told her. "I can't climb six steps without thinking I'm going to fall. And even if I was the right person for the job, it's not as easy as that. For instance," he gestured up at the invisible wall of rock, "you should never climb at night. It's one of the climbers' commandments." He remembered Mum telling him that, when he used to help her prepare her equipment in the kitchen.

Nettle came closer. "So you do know about climbing, then." There was an eagerness in her voice that he needed to squash.

"No! All I know is we'd only fall and kill ourselves if we went up now."

"Be brave, Max," Nettle persisted. Whether or not she could see his tears, she wouldn't let him off. "Bill said you could be brave. It's time to start!"

"I can't! Bill was wrong. We cannot climb this mountain!" They'd die, just like Mum had. He knew it.

"What about Wild?" Nettle must have got tired of playing good cop because she grabbed his shoulders and shook him, suddenly fierce again. "There may have been no one like your mum, but there's no one like Wild either. There's no one like my little brother! And he's still alive! I can't stop now. I *have* to keep going. I have to find the Shining Pathway. It must be around here somewhere. I'm going to find it, Max, whether you come with me or not!"

With a rustle of leaves, Nettle stumbled away from him.

"Wait!" He couldn't be separated from her now. Whatever he thought of her, whatever she thought of him, Nettle was his only link with the real world and he wanted to hang on to that at all costs. He tried to follow her but it was pitch black now and he didn't know which way to go. "Nettle! Where are you?"

She didn't answer. He stood still, listening hard. Standing alone like that, at the foot of the vast mountain, Max felt he was no better than a tiny, helpless ant. Fear and the night enveloped him. "Nettle! Please come back!"

"Tee hee! Can't catch me!"

He was just wondering why she had chosen this moment to taunt him like that when he realised that it wasn't Nettle who was speaking.

"Can't catch me!"

Following the sound of the voice, he looked up and saw the silhouette of the gingerbread man. He was clinging to the rock face, holding up a tiny lantern – no bigger than an acorn – in one pudgy hand.

"Can't catch me!" he rasped again.

"Stop that!" Nettle hissed, suddenly next to Max again. She could only have managed a few paces before the darkness had overwhelmed her too. "Why are you saying that?" she shouted, venting her feelings on the gingerbread man. "You always were the most stupid, irritating story character! What use are you?"

Max remembered how the gingerbread man kept running away from the people who had made him, until finally he was eaten by a fox. Of all the stories he knew, it was the one that made the least sense. It made no sense now either. The gingerbread man was going the wrong way. He should have been trying to get to Happy End, like everyone else.

"I'm the gingerbread man!" the biscuit chirped, as if that answered anything. Then he seemed to lose his footing and he dropped the lantern.

It fell at Max's feet. He picked it up quickly. "Wait!" he

shouted, raising the green light as high as he could above his head. "Are you OK?" But the gingerbread man had disappeared.

"He must have a death wish," Max said. He began to lower the lantern but Nettle nudged his arm.

"Glow-worms!" she said.

Max almost dropped the lantern when he saw what she meant. It wasn't a real lantern but a cluster of tiny bugs. There must have been over fifty of them, each one giving off a glowing green light. Part of him wanted to throw them away from him, but a bigger part was relieved to have something to see by, so he held on. He took a few tentative steps away from the mountain. He felt drained by fear and emotion: he needed a place to sit down and think for a minute. His head scraped against something rough. Quickly he lifted the lantern to see what it was. To his surprise he found he was standing in a porch. He had scuffed his head on the curved edge of a thatched roof which hung over a little wooden door.

"What is it?" Nettle said at his elbow.

"Looks like a cottage. But what's it doing here?" They hadn't passed a house for miles. Who could possibly want to live here? Max couldn't think of a single reason for building a house at the bottom of Harsh Mountain.

"I don't know," Nettle said. "But look."

Max saw that the door was open a crack, and a dim light was coming from inside.

"Should we go in?" Nettle said. "There might be food in there."

"Or beds," said Max. He'd give anything to lie down for a few minutes on a soft bed, and his stomach was aching with hunger. He had a sudden thought. "Hang on. What if it's the Three Bears' cottage?" If three angry bears attacked them now that would be the end of the quest; he didn't think he'd even have the strength to run away.

"I'm not scared of bears," Nettle said. "I'd rather meet three of them than those three chicken feet."

She had a point. In any case, Max thought, the chance of finding food and shelter from the dark night was so tempting, it was stronger than his fear. They looked at each other. Then, very gently, Max pushed the door further open and they went inside.

Max jumped as he saw a dark figure standing by the wall.

"Someone's here!" he hissed, backing up.

"Wait," Nettle whispered. She took the glow-worm lantern and held it up to show that the figure was only a hooded cape, hanging on a row of pegs.

They were in a kitchen with a long table. There was no one about, but a candle was burning on a shelf. It couldn't be the Three Bears' house because there were lots of chairs, and they were all the same size.

"Seven dwarves?" Max whispered.

Nettle shook her head.

"Too many places," she whispered back. There were eight chairs in total, all tucked neatly under the table. Max trembled as he realised there could be eight people in this house. How would they react if they found two strangers in their kitchen? Max would have to explain that they weren't burglars, but would he be able to do it in time, before they hit him and Nettle over the head with pokers or candlesticks?

"Look over here," Nettle said, carefully lifting the lid of a saucepan on the stove. "There's soup. It's still warm!" She put in a finger and sucked it. Max thought of fairy tales in which children ate things that made them shrink or grow huge, but before he knew it he found himself putting his finger in the soup and tasting it too. It was delicious.

Nettle picked up the ladle and they took turns to slurp the tepid soup from it. It tasted so fantastic that for a minute Max forgot about everything else except eating. Nettle scooped up more of the soup and they passed the ladle back and forth, more and more quickly.

Too quickly. In her keenness to eat, Nettle let go of the pan lid. It slipped and clattered noisily on the iron stove.

"Snow? That you, Snow?"

They both froze.

A very short man in a nightshirt and nightcap was standing in a doorway. The wire frames of his glasses glinted in the light of the candle he held in front of him.

He came closer and Max gasped as he held his candle up to their faces.

"Please don't hit us!" Max begged.

"You're not Snow." The man drew back the candle. "What are you two doing here?" He scratched his bearded chin. He didn't look angry. Max thought he saw disappointment in his eyes.

"Sorry," Max stammered. "So sorry." The man only came up to his shoulder but he was still scared of what he might do to them. "We're very tired, you see, and very hungry. We've been walking for hours."

"And your soup is so good," Nettle added. "Is it . . . is it leek and potato?"

The man nodded, seeming pleased. "I do a good leek and potato. The best in the world, Snow always said."

Who was Snow? Was the man talking about Snow White after all? Max flinched as the man suddenly turned, but he was only reaching for a basket of bread rolls. "Here. You can wipe the pan out with these."

Max took a roll and bit into its crusty shell. The fluffy white bread tasted like heaven. "Mm. Lovely. Thanks," he said.

The man watched as they cleaned the pan. It was hard to tell what he was thinking.

"I wasn't expecting visitors," he said after a while. "We don't see many new people out here. You lost, are you? Where you from?"

"Not exactly lost," Max answered. He felt he owed the man some sort of explanation. "We're from the Other World." That's what Bill Fairfoul had called it. "A place called Mansley. We came in a cake but then we met this wolf, Bill, and now we . . . we . . ." He couldn't go on; the whole story was too awful to say out loud.

"We're on our way to Beyond," Nettle said for him. "To fight Babs Haggard and rescue my little brother. Then we're going back to Mansley."

The man sucked his teeth. "You don't want to go to Beyond. No one's ever come back from there."

"We will," Nettle said firmly. Max wished he could be so sure.

The man didn't answer, just set his mouth in a straight line, like a minus sign.

"I wouldn't go getting mixed up with Babs Haggard if I were you. That witch would do anything. I'm Loth, by the way."

"Pardon?" Max said, his mouth full of the yummy, soggy bread.

"Loth," the man repeated. "You'll have heard of me. I'm one of the eight dwarves. We're the ones who took care of Snow White." He straightened his back. "I'm the tallest one, actually."

"*Eight* dwarves? I thought there were only seven."

A cloud seemed to pass over the man's face.

"I could be wrong," Max added hurriedly. "I'm not that up on stories." He looked to Nettle for support.

"Snow White and the *Seven* Dwarves, it is, in my book," she said.

"And the film," Max said, and then wished he hadn't.

Loth neatened the salt and pepper pots that stood on the table, although they didn't need neatening. "Been forgotten, have I? I suppose it's because I stayed behind. I didn't go with them, you see, when they left."

"When who left?" Max said.

"Snow and the others, and the prince. They went to Happy End, to get away. The witch has been putting the squeeze on us, you see. There's been no sunlight to speak of. Snow thought it would be safer in Happy End."

Max glanced at the solitary cape on the row of pegs. He remembered the man and woman he had hidden from in the foxgloves by the river. The seven hooded children hadn't been children after all. They were the seven dwarves.

"Just as well, in a way," Loth went on. "Not enough food here to go round now. The hens have been laying stones instead of eggs. All our crops have failed. I've only got a few leeks and the odd pumpkin left."

Max wiped his mouth, suddenly even more guilty about eating the man's food.

"Why didn't you leave too?" Nettle asked. "Why aren't you trying to get to Happy End? You could be a lot safer there."

Max wondered if she was right about that.

Loth made a face. "I was going to go, but then I decided against. I mean, I've never been out of this house. Lived here all my life. I didn't know what to expect. And someone's got to look after the place, haven't they?"

He reached up and pulled the thickest cobwebs Max had ever seen from a doorway.

"You two had best stay the night," said Loth. "Plenty of room. I'll sleep in the kitchen."

"We can't stay." Nettle dropped the ladle back in the pan. "Thanks for the food, but we can't waste any more time. We've got to get to Beyond. Haven't we, Max? We've got to find the Shining Pathway."

Max didn't meet her eye. For the first time in ages, he felt warm and almost safe. And he was so tired. He just wanted to lie down and rest and forget about the quest for a while. Now that he was in this cottage, he couldn't bear to leave it.

To his relief, Loth said, "You can't do anything now. No one can climb mountains or fight witches in the middle of the night. Besides, the Shining Pathway doesn't shine at night."

"Then it really does exist!" Nettle said. She grabbed Max's arm, looking almost joyful.

"Oh yes," Loth went on. "But like I said, it's not shining now. Follow me."

"We can't stay," Nettle said again, but Max could tell she

hadn't really got the energy to fight. Her eyes were drooping with tiredness. Now that he had warmed up and had food inside him, he could hardly keep his eyes open either.

Loth led the way to the bedroom, which was more like a dormitory – with little beds all lined up in a row. Max helped Loth push three of them together. Loth looked at Nettle and patted the three beds. She lay down straightaway, for once in her life doing what someone else told her to do. Loth arranged a grey flowered sheet over her, folding it back carefully in a neat line.

"We've got to go on," she said. "Got to." Her eyes were unnaturally bright, Max saw, like someone with a fever.

"Yes, yes," Loth soothed as he tucked her in.

Max took another group of beds and Loth passed him a woollen blanket. It was a huge relief to lie down. He lay on his back with his blistered feet sticking out from under the blanket, wondering if he'd ever be able to get up again.

"Max," Nettle murmured, "we've got to keep going. The Shining Pathway. It exists!"

"I know," Max said. "But we have to wait. In the morning. We'll find it in the morning."

She seemed half crazed with exhaustion and anxiety, and he expected her to argue, but when he looked over, Nettle's eyes were already closed.

"We'll find it in the morning, Nettle," he said again. She'd seemed so tense, almost delirious. He wanted her to hear something comforting as she went to sleep. But he didn't know if he meant what he said. No one could climb mountains or fight witches at night. Loth had told them that. But Max felt certain he couldn't do it in daylight either. If only he hadn't said that stupid thing in the cake about being an expert. It was all such a dreadful mistake.

He stayed awake for a while longer, listening as Loth padded around, drawing curtains, collecting blankets for himself before settling in an armchair in the kitchen. After that, all Max could hear was Nettle, breathing and sighing in her sleep.

Why me? Max thought for the millionth time, as in his mind's eye a stream of cakes, wolves, witches and mountains loomed into view. He tried to make them go away by thinking about his marble run instead, but the marble run wouldn't come to mind. What came instead was an image of Babs Haggard's terrifying face, her mouth stretched wide in triumphant laughter. And as Max fell helplessly into sleep, Pinocchio's sharp little voice stabbed its way into his dreams. *Babs Haggard is a lovely person. She's never killed or eaten anyone. Eaten, eaten . . .* it echoed. *She's never eaten anyone!*

⚡ Chapter Thirteen ⚡

Max woke from a deep sleep to feel warm, golden sunlight on his face. He kept his eyes closed for a moment. Maybe when he opened them he would be in bed, at home, next to his marble run. Maybe the witch, Wild's kidnapping and this whole quest thing would have been nothing more than a horrendous dream.

No such luck.

Opening his eyes he saw that the golden effect was created by his wedding cape, which had rucked up in the night and was covering his face. He pulled it away.

A dim morning light crept under the curtains. He was still in the dwarves' bedroom. Nettle was sound asleep on her row of beds, the flowered cover was thrown back and she had her arms flung up around her head. The frown he was so used to seeing on her face was smoothed away by sleep and she looked almost friendly. If only she could be like that when she was awake.

He gazed around the room. There was hardly any furniture. The walls were bare apart from one, which had an ornate mirror hanging on it, quite high up. Twirling flowers, hearts and birds decorated its frame, and there was a motto written underneath it in curly handwriting that he couldn't quite make out in the low light.

Limping because of his blisters, he went over and stood under the mirror. The glass was so scratched and tarnished he could hardly see his own reflection in it, but the motto was clear.

"Mirror mirror, up above," he read the words quietly under his breath, "show me, show me who I love."

As soon he finished speaking all the scratches disappeared, the glass cleared and there, in the mirror, as if by magic, was his mum. It wasn't just a photo of her, either. She was really there, smiling at him and nodding from inside the mirror. Her red hair bounced around her chin, just the way he remembered.

And her face wasn't a blur like it was whenever he tried to recall it. It was all there, perfect, as if she was just on the other side of a window.

"Max," she mouthed. Little lines crinkled at the corners of her eyes as she looked right at him.

"Mum," he said. "Mum."

He could hardly even speak. He couldn't believe how clearly he was seeing her. And there was so much he wanted to tell her, he didn't know where to begin.

He took his marbles out of his pocket and held them up for her to see.

"Still got these, look, Mum. Haven't even opened them. They're just the same as when you gave them to me."

Then he realised Mum was speaking too – very quietly, as if she was miles away – but he could hear what she said. She didn't seem to notice the marbles.

"There's a whole world out there, Max."

He loved the sound of her voice. It was a little bit husky with the beginnings of a laugh in it.

"Always try your hardest. Get stuck in to life and remember – never say never." That's what she'd always said to him. He'd forgotten that. "Oh yes, and don't save anything for best." She smiled. "There's no one like you, Max. I've always said it. You're one on your own. And there's a whole world out there waiting for you, love."

She winked at him. That wink made his heart feel as if it was melting.

"I . . . Mum . . ."

She was already fading over.

"No, wait!"

He went to touch the mirror to try to call her back, just

as Dad appeared. He was sitting at a table in his wedding clothes. Ilona was there too. She had her arms around him. She shouldn't be there, Max thought with a pang. The magic mirror was showing him the people he loved. Ilona didn't belong there. Her hair was dangling in Dad's champagne glass, but neither she nor Dad noticed that. They were both smiling out at Max.

"Are you OK, Dad?" he whispered. "Have you got your inhaler? Please don't worry about me. I'm coming back. Soon as I can get out of this place."

Dad and Ilona waved and began to fade too, like Mum had. Max thought the mirror had finished showing him things then, so it was a surprise when Nettle appeared in the oval space vacated by Dad and Ilona. Max spun round, expecting to see her standing there. But she wasn't behind him. She was still sleeping on her three little beds.

"Come on, Max!" the Nettle in the mirror said, putting her hands on her hips. He'd seen the real Nettle do that plenty of times. Only this Nettle was grinning at him, as if she liked him. The mirror had got that completely wrong. Nettle never smiled at him and, although he had started to get on better with her recently, she wasn't special to him, not like Mum and Dad were.

Then Nettle's image was replaced too, by another, much more alarming one.

This time it was Wild. He appeared to be clutching the bars of a cage, and he looked shivery and scared.

"Help me, Maxi-Nettle," he said, his little face squeezed between two iron bars. "Help me."

"Wild!" Max gripped the mirror. "What's happening? Where are you?"

Wild looked to one side with wide eyes and seemed to shrink back, as if he was afraid of whoever or whatever was approaching. Max pressed his nose to the mirror, trying to see more, but then the glass clouded over, and Wild disappeared from view.

"We're coming, Wild, we're coming!" He knew he probably couldn't hear him – the mirror's communication system seemed to be a one-way thing – but Max desperately wanted to try and reassure Wild that they were close. They were still coming.

The mirror had returned to its original state now, and all Max could see in its cracked surface was his own shocked reflection and, behind him, Loth's still one.

"You found the mirror, then," Loth said. "I look in there every day to see Snow White. Sometimes more than once."

Max touched the mirror frame. He didn't want Loth to see he was trembling. "I think . . . I think your mirror might have a technical fault," he said. He'd seen Mum and Dad in it. But he'd seen Ilona too, and Nettle and Wild. He didn't *love* any of them. Why had the mirror shown them to him?

"The mirror never lies," Loth said. "It shows you people you've loved, people you love now and people you're going to love in the future. It only ever shows me Snow, though. I'm devoted to her, I am."

He took a step forward. "I've been thinking. You can stay here if you like, Max. Stay as long as you want. I've plenty of room."

Max was standing still, struggling to take in the full meaning of what Loth had just said. Loth must have taken his silence as encouragement because he fixed his eyes on Max's in the mirror and spoke in a voice as soothing as a lullaby, "No one could blame you for staying put. You're like me, you see. I can tell. You're afraid. But you don't have to go. There's no need for you to go anywhere at all."

"No!" Max tore himself away from the mirror and whipped round. He didn't know what he'd been thinking before. Of course he couldn't stay in this cottage. Nothing good could come of that. The mirror had made it clear to him. He had to get out of here at once and start saving Wild.

"You don't understand," he told Loth. "Someone I love, or someone I'm going to love very soon, is in terrible danger. Something terrible is about to happen to my new brother. I can't just sit here and let that happen!"

Hearing his raised voice, Nettle woke. She sat up at once. "What is it? What's going on?"

Max rushed over to her. "Hurry up, Nettle. Get up. We've got to go. We've got to go now!"

She didn't need telling twice. "That's what I've been saying all along." She wrenched off the flowered coverlet, swung out of bed and went to grab her shoes from the rack by the door, where Loth had placed them the night before.

"Can Max borrow these?" She held up a pair of tall black boots with criss-crossing laces.

"Those are Snow's." Loth took them from her and stroked the shiny leather.

"Right," Nettle said. "But she's not here, is she? And Max is. And he hasn't got any shoes. So can he use them?"

Loth hugged the boots to him. "They're good ones," he said. "I've been keeping them polished." He hesitated. "But I suppose if she was here, Snow would say we should lend them to you."

Reluctantly, he passed them to Max.

"Thanks!" Max pulled the boots on at once, yanking the laces tight. He glanced gratefully at Nettle. The boots fitted perfectly and they were so comfortable it didn't matter if they were a girl's. They would help him reach Wild faster and he realised that was all he cared about now.

He and Nettle ran, jostling for the front door. Max let her through first and turned, remembering his manners. "Thanks for the food and everything."

But Loth was peering into the mirror, mumbling at whatever he could see there.

"I think she made it, by the way," Max said. "I think Snow White made it to Happy End. If that helps." Loth didn't reply, but Max was pretty sure he heard, because he smiled, ever so slightly, into the mirror.

Max took one last look around the gloomy cottage. All of it tidy, all of it dusty and grey and draped with cobwebs. Then he ran out after Nettle, pulling the door shut behind him.

As he charged away, Max felt sorry for Loth, but he knew he owed him too. Not just for the food and the bed for the night. There was more to it than that. Loth had shown Max something. He had shown him a way of being that Max knew now he didn't want any part of. He didn't want to be like Loth. He didn't want to be the one left alone in a silent cottage, gathering dust. He wanted to be out doing things, just like Mum had said. *Try your hardest*, she'd told him from the mirror. *Get stuck in*. And if that meant taking risks, even big ones, then so be it. From now on, getting stuck in was exactly what he was going to do.

Chapter Fourteen

Max hurtled along with so much stamina he thought he could run for miles if necessary. He felt completely different. Until this moment he'd felt as if he was being dragged along through Ever After against his will. He'd done things because he had to, because if he didn't do them he'd never stand a chance of getting home. But now he was a boy on a mission. He was a boy with people to care about, people to save. And he was full of new energy.

He caught up with Nettle almost immediately. She hadn't got very far. She was standing with her head thrown back, staring upwards.

"Oh, Max," she whispered.

Last night, in the dark, they had only sensed Harsh Mountain, and touched it. This morning, in the dim light of the sickly sun, they could see it too, in all its terrible glory. The mountain was so tall the summit wasn't visible from where they stood. It was as steep and sheer as a cliff, and the rock was perfectly smooth, with no sign of a single foothold.

"You were right, Max. We'll never get up it."

Max put his hands on his hips, scanning the rock. "Never say never."

Nettle stared. "What did you just say?"

"Never say never. You know what that means, don't you?"

"I understand the words all right. I just never thought I'd hear them coming out of *your* mouth."

"Well." Max smiled. "First time for everything, I suppose."

Nettle snorted as if to say she'd never expected to hear *those* words coming out of Max's mouth either.

She studied him curiously. "Are you the real Max?" she asked. "Or did some gremlins come and swap you in the night?"

"Nothing like that," Max said. He was rather enjoying the effect he was having on her. "I just feel differently now, that's all. Sometimes the things that seem impossible at night seem a lot more possible when daylight comes. Don't you think?"

And before she could reply, he said, "Come on, Nettle. Let's get moving. We've got to find the Shining Pathway." He ran along by the side of the immense mountain, shouting at the top of his voice, "Show yourself, Shining Pathway! Show yourself!" He had to shout. He was so fired up; he had more energy this morning than he knew what to do with. "Show yourself! Show yourself!" he cried, and his voice echoed back at him.

They kept running, faster and faster, until Max's yellow cape flew upwards. The brightness of the material fluttering around his shoulders made him suddenly aware that he and Nettle were the only colourful things in the landscape now. The sky was grey as week-old porridge; the sun was beige instead of yellow, and it seemed to wobble unsteadily, as if it knew it only had the strength to rise one more time. If they didn't stop her, Babs Haggard would soon achieve her aim of blotting out all the colour and joy from the Land of Ever After, and all the daylight too. And who knew what she would do to Wild.

Suddenly Max glimpsed something else that was bright.

"Look there!" he said, pointing through the murk to a streak of brilliant white stretching down the mountain. It looked like a frothing waterfall, a glacier perhaps, or a long fall of snow.

"The Shining Pathway!" Nettle breathed. "It must be!" She clutched Max's arm. "We've found it!"

They moved on, their eyes locked onto the shimmering stream of white. Max was afraid that if either of them took their eyes off it for so much as a second it might disappear. He didn't even want to blink.

At last they reached it. It wasn't water, or ice, or even snow. It lay against the mountain in long strands, like a fringed scarf.

"What is this stuff?" Max said. He hadn't known what to expect but he hadn't expected this.

"I don't know." Nettle picked up a white strand. "It feels like silk." She stroked her cheek with it. "It's beautiful."

"Thank you for the compliment!" a faraway voice tinkled.

They turned, but there was no one about.

"Up here, sillies!" the voice called. They looked up, craning their necks, but they still couldn't see anyone. "Make haste. I've let my hair down for you, haven't I? Come on up!"

"Rapunzel!" Nettle said, and Max said it too, almost immediately after her. He was recognising story characters almost as quickly as she was now. The Shining Pathway, he realised, was Rapunzel's hair. And it was to be their way up Harsh Mountain.

Max took hold of a tress of the hair and pulled on it, the way he'd seen Mum do when she was checking a rope. It felt very strong. Nettle grabbed another tress and pulled herself upwards, but the shining hair was too slippery to be gripped like rope and she slid straight to the ground and landed on her back.

"It's not working," she said. "How are we going to use it to get all the way up there?"

"Chop chop, you two!" Rapunzel's voice rang out.

Max stared at the hair. They could try plaiting it, but even then it would still be too soft and slippery to hold on to. He searched for some other solution, determined not to let his new positive feelings slip away. They couldn't be defeated by this, not with Wild waiting on the other side of the mountain. He thought again of the boy's little face, pressed between the bars of a cage. He couldn't tell Nettle what he'd seen in the mirror. It would only make it worse for her.

"I know!" he said at last, snapping his fingers as the idea came to him. "We can make a harness."

He gathered the hair in his arms and made a large loop with it. He twisted the hair and tied it into itself in a big bowline knot. Mum had taught him how to do knots. He'd spent ages with her in the kitchen, helping prepare her ropes and safety equipment. He hadn't done a bowline for years but, strangely, his fingers seemed to remember exactly how to do it. He worked quickly, making sure to add a stopper knot at the end of the rope of hair to prevent the bowline from slipping out and dropping them.

Nettle watched him work. "Now what?" she said, licking her lips nervously.

"Now we climb in," he said.

Nettle looked terrified but she gritted her teeth and stepped into the loop of hair. "How do you know it will hold?"

"It will." Max stepped in next to her. He tried to sound more confident than he felt. He'd dreaded this moment, but now that it had come he kept busy concentrating on the practicalities. That way his brain didn't have space for too much fear. He just hoped he was doing the right thing.

He arranged the thick hair so it spread out underneath them, like a swing seat.

"Ready?" Rapunzel called from above.

Max gave the hair-rope a brief tug. They were secure, or as secure as they could be without proper safety harnesses or crash helmets. "Ready!" he called.

"How will she hold our weight, though?" Nettle clutched anxiously at the hair as their feet left the ground.

"I'll wind you up here!" came the reply from above. "I've got a winch. The handle's stiff, but I reckon I can manage it. Hold tight!"

They moved upwards, jerkily at first, then more smoothly and faster.

Max kept his eyes closed as they rose. There was nothing either of them could do; they just had to trust in Rapunzel. Max had never even met her but something in her confident voice made him believe that if she said she could bring them up the mountain, then she could. And at least there was no actual climbing involved.

He felt himself whizzing rapidly upwards through the air.

He was doing it! He was actually going up Harsh Mountain. He wasn't making the ascent in the way he'd expected and he was still terrified of what lay on the other side of the mountain, but for better or worse, he was on his way to Beyond.

"Here you are at last!"

Max's feet met a ledge and he opened his eyes. He tried not to look down. He could tell that they were very high up because the temperature had dropped dramatically and his eyes were level with a dark grey cloud.

"Well done us! I knew we'd do it!" Someone was peering at them from behind a metal grid, which was pressed into the rock. To his surprise it was a bent and frail-looking old woman, who was jumping up and down like a girl.

"Still got my strength, you see." A pair of shining blue eyes twinkled at them out of the woman's lined and leathery face. "I knew I'd be able to haul you up."

"How did you know we were coming?" Nettle asked, a little shakily.

"I've been watching your progress," Rapunzel said. "I can see everything from up here. It's the only good thing about this prison."

"Did Babs Haggard put you in there?" Max asked, trying to see into the woman's tiny mountain prison. It was no better than a dank cave.

"Need you ask? She hated me because of my beauty, and

150

my hair. It used to be a lovely red colour. She was jealous as anything, so she put me in here and she did this to me."

Rapunzel put out a slim hand which was wrinkled and covered in brown spots, and stroked a strand of her hair. "She's turned it white now. I'm an old, old lady, way before my time. Babs Haggard is so evil. I can't wait for her to be defeated." She narrowed her eyes at them. "You have come to defeat her, haven't you?"

"Yes," Max said. "We have. We're going to rescue our little brother too."

Nettle stared at him. "*Our* little brother?"

He stared back. He hadn't known he was going to say that. It had just slipped out; but it still felt right. "Yes," he said. "Yours and mine."

Nettle's mouth twitched at the corners, as if she might be about to smile, or maybe cry.

"Well, if you're going to do all that, you'd better hurry up." Rapunzel nodded at the view. "Because I'll tell you what: you haven't come a moment too soon!"

Still holding tight to Rapunzel's hair, Max and Nettle dared to look back.

Rapunzel was right. They could see all the land they'd crossed. The valleys, the plains, the river and the woods. The Land of Ever After looked much worse than when they had travelled through it. Everything was completely grey now. Nothing grew. No people walked. No animals roamed.

No birds flew in the sky. There was nothing and no one to be seen. With Lord Malberry and his magic gone, Babs Haggard had been free to do her worst. There didn't seem to be a single thing that hadn't been overwhelmed by her evil.

Max peered into the distance, searching for signs of life in Happy End. He could just make out the top of the palace. Its drooping flags had fallen off now, and its chimneys and turrets were starting to crumble. He recognised the ridge of Giant Fell in front of it. A huge tree seemed to be growing out of it.

"I don't remember that—" He broke off and gasped as Nettle touched his wrist, seeing what he was seeing. It wasn't a tree, although it was as thick as the trunk of a massive oak. It was the giant's arm, raised up in the air with a huge clenched fist on top. The giant was still lying down but it wouldn't be long before he was up, and wreaking havoc. They were running out of time. Max had no idea how he could turn all this around. He didn't know how to fight such immense power – but he'd come this far, and at least now he was determined to try.

"Here. You'll need this to get down the other side."

Rapunzel's face disappeared and was immediately replaced by a rolled-up carpet which she stuffed through the grid. "This'll make the way down to Beyond a bit more comfortable for you."

"What do you mean?" Nettle said as she took the carpet from her. Max realised he had been so worried about climbing the mountain, he hadn't even considered how to get down the other side.

"Oh, you'll see when you reach the top. Go on. It's only a short scramble from here."

"What about you?" Nettle said. "Shouldn't we try and let you out?"

"That will take too long," Rapunzel answered. "Don't worry about me. I've been here for months so I can wait another few hours. You can let me out on your way back."

"No one's ever come back from Beyond," Nettle said. "That's what we've been told." Max had never heard her sound so doubtful.

"There's always a first time," Rapunzel said. "With a bit of luck, this is that time."

"Never say never," Max murmured, as he and Nettle dropped to their hands and feet. They pushed the rolled carpet in front of them and clambered to the very top of the mountain.

Max was trembling almost uncontrollably when they reached the summit. He got carefully to his feet, placed his hands on his thighs to stop his legs from shaking, and took a long, deep breath. He had done it. He hadn't believed it possible, but somehow he and Nettle had done it. They had reached the top of Harsh Mountain. Nettle stood up beside him and together they looked down on Babs Haggard's domain. Max could clearly see what lay ahead. And it was more horrible than he could ever have imagined.

It was Beyond.

Chapter Fifteen

If the land before Harsh Mountain had looked grey and dead, the land on the other side was deader still. The blackened earth of Beyond was flat, and as barren as if it had been coated in volcanic lava. Icy winds whistled and blew across the bleak, forbidding wasteland.

As far as Max could tell, there was only one thing in the whole place. A gigantic building surrounded by a wide maze of dense black hedges. It was the scariest building Max had ever seen. It was round with a hole in the centre, like a huge, decaying doughnut. The circular structure had almost no windows and its walls were as black as thick bin bags. Drains and pipes ran and corkscrewed their way over its exterior, in some complicated system of outdoor plumbing.

The building must be Babs Haggard's palace. It was the

headquarters of evil, and Wild was somewhere inside it.

Max and Nettle stood clutching the carpet Rapunzel had given them, trying to steady themselves against the vicious wind. It still wasn't clear to Max how they were supposed to get down.

"Can't catch me!" a tiny voice carried on the wind.

Max dared to lean out a little and saw a tall column of rock, stretching up as high as the mountain top. It was a cliff stack, like the ones Mum sometimes climbed, and it was connected to Harsh Mountain by a narrow stone bridge. An impossibly steep path corkscrewed its way around the stack. And going down it, whirling round and round as if he was on a helter-skelter at a funfair, was the gingerbread man. His tiny hands waved above his head.

"Whee! Can't catch me!"

How did he get here? Max wondered. "Is he following us or something?" he yelled into Nettle's ear, battling to make himself heard above the shrieking wind.

"Maybe," she yelled back. She tapped the carpet. "But I think I know what this is for now." And Max knew immediately what she meant.

They didn't talk about what they were going to do. Talking might lead to doubts and there was no longer any time for those. They only had twenty-four hours left, perhaps less. The poor sun didn't look as if it had the energy for even one more sunrise.

Pushing his fears of falling to the very back of his mind, Max helped Nettle lift the carpet. Working together, they tucked it as firmly as they could under their right arms and prepared to cross the stone bridge. One false move to either side, one sudden change in the wind direction, and they would fall, plunging thousands of feet to certain death. Max felt as if his legs didn't belong to him as he forced himself forward, focusing on matching Nettle step for step for step.

Once over, they stood, breathing fast, shocked at what they had just done. They weren't safe yet, though, not by any means. The path that led down the cliff stack was so steep, it was almost perpendicular in places. This was no helter-skelter ride. Still panting, they spread out the carpet.

Nettle sat down on the carpet and Max sat behind her, his arms around her waist. Normally he would have felt far too self-conscious to do that, but this was a matter of life and death. They pushed off with their feet and the carpet slid and whirled round and round the stack. Clinging to one another, Max and Nettle lay back, flattening themselves against the carpet, trying desperately not to be thrown off the cliff stack. Faster and faster they went, bumping over ice moguls and stony mounds, going at such a terrific speed that the rock and the sky blurred together as they tore by.

They reached the bottom in a matter of seconds. There was no way of braking and they went somersaulting helplessly, rolling away from the stack, and each other, like a pair of tiny coins dropped from a giant's purse. Finally they came to a halt and lay, winded and gasping, on the ground.

As soon as he could, Max sat up. Amazingly, he wasn't hurt – he was hardly even bruised. He felt so exhilarated by the climb and then the slide that he burst out laughing. He wasn't dead! "Hey, Nettle, we did it! We got over Harsh Mountain!"

"Oh no!"

Nettle was sitting up a few metres off, turned away from him, her hands pressed to her mouth.

"What is it?" Max went over to see what she was looking at.

It was the gingerbread man. Or rather, what was left of him. His grey body lay face down on the ground. It was broken clean in half and his little legs were crushed to crumbs.

"Wild!" Nettle's eyes were full of tears. "Wild!"

"It's not him," Max said. "It's only a biscuit, Nettle." He put his hands on her shoulders and tried to comfort her. "It's not Wild." He knew it wasn't a real boy, but it was still a shock to see something that had been running and talking lying so broken and still.

"I know it's not Wild!" Nettle said, crying out. "But it could be him. It soon could be!"

"We're not going to let it be. Come on." Max moved away

but Nettle held back, still gazing at the broken gingerbread man.

"Why did he keep running like that?" she said. "He wore himself out. Why did he never stop when we asked him to?"

And why did he come here anyway, Max thought, when everyone else was trying to get to Happy End? He stared at the body. One arm was still flung out as if it was pointing, pointing into Beyond.

And it came to him. Max realised he knew exactly why the gingerbread man was here and why he had kept appearing to them.

"He was showing us the way!" he said. "He wasn't taunting us. He was trying to help us!"

Nettle gazed at him. Then she nodded slowly. "Of course," she said. "Of course he was." She went and touched the gingerbread body, gently stroking its back. "He helped us, Max. I think we should do something for him too. Leave something."

"Pay our respects?" Max said. Although he didn't know how. They couldn't bury him. The ground was too hard and they had nothing to dig with. He remembered that when sailors were buried at sea, they were wrapped in their country's flag and thrown into the water.

Thinking of that, he unpinned his yellow cape and passed it to Nettle. She seemed to understand and know what to do. She stepped forward and laid the cape gently over the body. Max stepped forward too and used the brooch to secure the cape as best he could against the wind. He hadn't done anything like this at Mum's funeral, he thought, as he pushed the pin of the brooch into the ground. He hadn't done anything at all then. Dad had wanted him to help put the flowers on her coffin but he'd refused. He hadn't wanted to do it, because he didn't want to believe she was really dead. One day Mum was there, packing her stuff up in the kitchen and singing, and the next she wasn't. It had been too hard to understand.

He knew now, though. He accepted it now. He bowed his head and he knew he was giving thanks, not just for the gingerbread man who had lost his life trying to help them, but also for Mum.

"Rest in peace, gingerbread man," Nettle said.

"Rest in peace," Max said, and then whispered it again, one more time. "Rest in peace." He put his hands in his pockets and his fingers enclosed the marble net.

Nettle tugged at his sleeve, but she did it gently, as if she understood he was thinking about his mum.

Together they backed away and moved on to the forbidding dark maze they'd seen from Rapunzel's prison lookout post.

Now that they were on the ground, Max could tell how tall the maze walls really were. There was no way of seeing over their tops, not even if one of them stood on the other's shoulders. And there was no climbing onto them either. The walls weren't made of living hedges, like the ones Max had seen before. They were hard metal, made up of dense rows of oily black chains. You couldn't see through them at all.

"We'll never get through!" Nettle said. "It's impossible!"

The funny thing was that Max didn't think so. The old Max might have agreed and given up, but the new Max, the one who had burst out of Loth's cottage full of determination, wasn't put off. A maze was just a puzzle, after all, and Max was pretty good at puzzles. He always did the ones in the back of *Construction Matters.* He was confident he could do this one too.

"We just have to make sure we stick together," he said, "and not get lost inside. It shouldn't take too long."

"What about coming back?" Nettle hesitated as they felt their way along the first narrow paths.

"Easy," Max said. "We'll use these." He took his marble net from his pocket.

"Your mum's marbles. Are you sure?"

Max stared at the marbles in his hand. He had hardly thought about it. He'd just got them out on the spur of the moment. That wasn't something he normally did. It had just felt like the right thing to do. He tossed the marbles up in the air and caught them again. Then, without giving himself time to change his mind, he ripped the net open.

"Yes. I am sure. I was keeping them for something else actually, but there's no point saving things for best."

He almost smiled, remembering how Mum had said that to him. It was odd. A day ago his marbles and his marble run had been the most precious things in his life, but he didn't feel like that any longer. Rescuing Wild and getting him out of Beyond was far, far more important.

They turned a corner and he set down the first marble as a marker. It was a milky white one and it showed up well in the dark passageway.

"Now we'll be able to retrace our steps."

Nettle nodded. "Just like Hansel and Gretel."

"Oh yes!" Max said. He hadn't thought of that.

He almost enjoyed solving the maze. He already had a rough idea of how it was constructed, having seen it from above, and all those puzzles he'd done in his magazines were paying off. He knew instinctively which way to go. Even though they were heading towards terrible danger, it was still satisfying, passing the marbles one at a time to Nettle for her to leave as a marker, each time they turned a crucial corner. Nettle seemed to trust him to pick the right moment to lay down each one. It struck him that she wouldn't have done that the day before. And as for Mum, she never could have guessed how he'd end up using her last gift to him. But he knew she would have been pleased he'd found such a good use for the marbles. He didn't get lost once.

When they turned the last corner, he had just one marble left. He put it away in his pocket and they came out into the open.

As soon as they stepped out of the maze a heavy cloud, dark as charcoal, rolled over the black palace towards them. It loomed over them, casting such a deep shadow that Nettle looked completely grey. Her clothes, her hair, everything about her, apart from her greenish-brown eyes, was grey. The shocked expression on her face told Max that the same thing had happened to him. It occurred to him that they were no different from the characters in Ever After. It didn't matter that they were from the "Other World", they were as susceptible to Babs Haggard's magic as everyone else.

The cloud rotated slowly and then began to shed its load. It wasn't rain that fell. It wasn't sleet, or even snow.

It was ash.

Cold, grey ash. It fell silently, in soft, damp clumps. Max slapped it from his shoulders and shook it from Snow White's boots. Nettle tossed her hair to get rid of it but it kept on falling.

Max saw Nettle open her mouth to say something to him but a thick curtain of ash dropped between them and he couldn't hear.

"What?"

Nettle used her hand to wipe ash from her tongue.

"The marbles!" she said, spitting dark grey saliva.

Max looked back. The paths of the maze were heaped with the falling ash. It was already up to knee height, and the cloud looked set to continue pouring ash until it had filled in the maze completely. They would never find the marbles again in all that. There would be no quick getaway after all.

Chapter Sixteen

Quick getaway or not, they had made it as far as Babs Haggard's headquarters. Wild was in there somewhere, and they had to find him.

As he and Nettle passed through the great iron gates, Max felt how very small they were, and how exposed. If Babs Haggard could see them already, they were no safer now than a pair of baby mice walking straight towards a hungry, hunting cat. Perhaps it was just as well that the two of them were as grey as their surroundings. The ash continued to fall, drifting up their noses and into their throats like bitter icing sugar, making them wheeze and cough, but at least it gave them some camouflage.

The whole palace seemed to be rotting away. Max had never seen a building so uncared for. The higgledy-piggledy drains and gutters he'd spotted from the top of the mountain were broken in many places. Water wheels, with missing spokes, turned slowly and dripped rusty water down the walls.

"Careful," Max warned as Nettle pulled on a creaking door. If the witch caught them here, their whole journey could have been for nothing.

Nettle looked back at him but she didn't stop. Max followed her through the door into a black-painted hall paved with dark, cracked marble. "Watch out for traps," he hissed. He was all too aware that the chicken feet could appear, disguised as anything, and at any time.

But Nettle's head was up and she walked swiftly, glancing from side to side. Max knew it was because she could sense Wild was close at last. She opened a door to her left, put her head round, and went straight through.

Max followed as she toured the rooms, scanning them for signs of Wild. Each room they entered was different from the one before. One was a dark and dirty cave, another a room full of sticky cobwebs, a third was lined with mirrors and otherwise empty, apart from a glassy black throne. The only thing the rooms had in common was their darkness, their curved shape and the fact that you wouldn't want to spend any more time in them than absolutely necessary.

Nettle passed through a series of archways, pulling at curtains, lifting lids of trunks and tearing at cobweb blankets. There was no sign of Wild.

"Where is he?" Nettle whispered, as they came into the entrance hall again. "Where is she hiding him?"

"I don't know," Max replied, realising they had gone round in a circle. "But we need to make a plan." He knew that anything they did now was going to be crucial. Their success or failure hinged on whatever action they took next. Just then, Nettle stopped him with a hand.

"Did you hear that?" she said.

Max hadn't heard anything. In fact, they'd hardly heard any sound at all since they'd arrived in Beyond. Everything had been silenced by the falling ash.

But now he did hear an odd, breathy little noise.

"It came from out there," Nettle whispered.

She hurried to the single window which opened, like a ship's porthole, onto the round courtyard in the centre of the doughnut palace.

"It's her! It's Babs Haggard!" She sank to the floor, then raised her head just high enough to peep out again.

Max dropped to the floor too, then crawled and peered over Nettle's shoulder.

The first thing he saw was the cauldron-chariot, parked on the perimeter of the courtyard. The three chicken feet sat next to it, as if awaiting their next instructions. Beside them was a grey, stone statue of a man, hunched over, holding a metal bucket.

In the centre of the courtyard was Babs Haggard herself.

She had her back to them and her spiny wings fluttered with excitement as she leaned over a cage.

A coldness swept through Max's stomach as he recognised the cage. Its bars were identical to the one he'd glimpsed in Loth's mirror.

"More din-dins, my plump little pheasant?" Babs Haggard said. "More of your delicious gravy?" She was holding a funnel with a tube attached and she was pressing it into the cage. "You'd like that, wouldn't you?"

Max wanted to grip Nettle's shoulder. He wanted to try and brace her for what he knew was about to come, but he couldn't move.

There was a burping sound and a familiar voice said, "No! 'Nuff gravy now. I'm full up."

"Wild!" Nettle whimpered.

Max reached out and put a steadying hand on her back.

"What's that, my little dumpling?" the witch said in mock surprise, putting a rake-like hand to her ear, pretending she hadn't heard. "You want thirds and fourths, too?"

As Babs Haggard stood back, Max and Nettle had their first proper sight of Wild. He was in the cage and he looked dreadful. He was still in his wedding nightie, which had a few feathers left on it, but apart from that he was almost unrecognisable. His face and his curly hair had turned grey and he was chubbier than before. It was only a day since they'd seen him, but his face had filled out so much his

168

cheeks looked as if they were stuffed with cotton wool. His expression was dull and slow. He couldn't have been less like himself.

The transformation in him was horrifying. Max couldn't imagine what Nettle must be feeling as her body trembled violently under his hand.

Wild seemed almost to be dropping off as Babs Haggard tapped her clawed foot. Gorging on gravy must be exhausting him. "I'm waiting," she said. "Thirds and fourths, is it? Or thirds and fourths and *fifths*?"

Wild came to suddenly, terrified at the mention of fifths. "Thirds and fourths," he stammered.

"There's my good juicy boy," Babs Haggard crooned. "POUR!" she barked, making Wild, Max and Nettle all jump in shock.

Nothing happened.

"Stark!" Babs Haggard screamed. "I said, *pour!*"

Very slowly, the hunched figure Max had mistaken for a statue stepped forward. Max realised that he and Nettle probably looked like statues too, since the ash fall. But this man was even greyer than they were. His grey eyelids were draped like heavy hoods over his eyes. He seemed drained not only of his colour, but also of his heart and his feelings. He looked as if Babs Haggard had sucked out his soul.

"Pour!" Babs Haggard jabbed the man with a vicious finger. That finger was sharp as a needle, but the man barely seemed to notice it. He lifted his bucket and poured a thick brown sludge into the waiting funnel. The mixture slopped and slid down the tube and glugged into Wild's mouth. He swallowed and swallowed and swallowed. Wild had once said that gravy was his favourite food. Max bet it wasn't any more. Just watching made him feel dreadfully sick.

At last Wild stopped swallowing and gulped for air instead.

"'Nuff gravy now, please, Bag Haggard," he begged.

"*Babs* Haggard," the witch corrected him, through gritted teeth. "But that was only your third helping, my sweet samosa," she went on, not even bothering to soften her tone of voice this time. "Stark. Pour again!"

Max couldn't bear to watch as the man raised the bucket. He took his hand off Nettle's back and he closed his eyes. But that was a big mistake, because as soon as he moved his hand she let out a huge, anguished wail. "*Wild!*"

"Maxi-Nettle!" Wild cried, seeing both their faces at the window. He clutched the bars of the cage in exactly the way Max had seen in Loth's mirror. "Maxi-Nettle. Help, Maxi-Nettle!"

The witch whirled round, wings whirring, her glittering black eyes revolving in their sockets. Her nose twitched about as she peered across the courtyard, trying to see what Wild had seen.

Max flung himself down out of sight, expecting Nettle to

do the same. To his dismay, she climbed up to the window and launched herself through it.

"No! Nettle. Don't!"

He was too late.

"Wild!" he heard Nettle cry. "It's all right, Wild, I'm here now! I'm here!"

It wasn't all right. It was the worst possible thing that could have happened. Max lay, crushing his hands into his face, dreading what might come next.

"Well, look at that," Babs Haggard's icy voice sliced through the air. "As if by magic, here comes the cavalry!"

Nettle was shouting, "You let him go, you horrible hag! Let him go!" She was obviously so distraught she'd even forgotten to be scared.

There was a pause. The witch didn't shout back. When she did speak, Max thought he detected amusement in her voice.

"I knew all I had to do was wait. I knew he wasn't alone. You sponge-hearted humans never seem to know when to give up on each other. My chicken feet may have failed to bring you to me, but I knew you'd make your own way eventually."

"You let my brother go! You let him go this minute!" Nettle sounded angry but her voice shook too, as if she was realising the enormity of what she had just done.

Max was terrified. He had to clutch his knees together

to stop them knocking as he listened to Babs Haggard's answer.

"Oh, don't worry about your brother, Maxi-Nettle," she put on her fake kind voice again, "I've given him nothing but care and attention, and lots and lots and *lots* of his favourite gravy. And he's in such great shape. Look at him. He's dimpled and fleshy, and tasty. I should say he's just about *oven-ready*, wouldn't you?"

Max felt as if he'd been kicked in the stomach. He'd half known it for some time, but it was still a terrible shock to hear that Babs Haggard really did mean to kill Wild. And eat him too!

Nettle was yelling now. "You're not eating my brother, you sick old witch. I won't let you!"

"Nonsense. Of course I'm going to eat him. I'm going to eat him for my victory breakfast. Tomorrow. And you, Maxi-Nettle, can be the waitress!"

Max heard Nettle give a kind of desperate war cry. There was no talking after that, just scraping and puffing, and he couldn't tell what was going on. He couldn't risk looking through the window again but he found a walnut-sized hole in the wall and dared to look through that instead.

He was amazed to see Nettle grappling with Babs Haggard. Nettle wasn't the most sensible person he knew but she was definitely the bravest. He saw her aim a hard punch right at the witch's nose. Babs Haggard's head flew back and one of her black eyes fell to the ground and rolled away. The witch looked mad, then she blinked really hard and another swirling eye popped up in place of the old one.

"Oh, you shouldn't have done that, my sweet," she said in a calm voice, full of threat.

Nettle was so shocked that she didn't move for a moment.

Max wanted to shout at her, to tell her to run. He knew he couldn't, though. If he gave himself away too, then there really wouldn't be any hope for them at all.

It was too late anyway. The witch had hold of Nettle again.

"Let go of me!" Nettle cried. "You let me go! I want to be with my brother!"

"Nothing simpler, Maxi-Nettle. It will be my pleasure to reunite you!" Babs Haggard opened the gate of the cage, thrust Nettle inside and slammed it shut.

Nettle hugged Wild hard, as if she'd never stop. "What's she done to you, Wild? Oh, I'm sorry, I'm so sorry."

"Want to go home now," Wild said slowly, resting his fat face against her shoulder. "Want Ilona. Feel too full. Feel sick."

"I know," Nettle comforted. "And we will. We will go home. We'll get you there. Soon. I promise."

Wild didn't look as if he believed her. He blinked and sucked his thumb. Max wasn't sure he believed her either. He couldn't see any way out of this.

The witch chuckled to herself and fluttered up on top of the cage.

"What a touching reunion!"

She stalked about over Nettle and Wild's heads.

"Well, my dears, it's coming up to bedtime, so I think I'll tell you a little story. That's what children enjoy, isn't it – a nice, soothing bedtime story."

"Stay here, Stark," she said sharply as the big grey man turned to leave. "I think you'd like to hear this story too. Because this story," she folded and clicked her rake hands, "is the story to end all stories!"

Max could only watch, mesmerised, as Babs Haggard sat down on the cage and arranged her skirts.

"Now I'm sitting comfortably," she said, "I'll begin. Once upon a time, a great witch decided she'd had enough of happiness and joy so she set out to remove them from the world. Of course, there was a protector of happiness and joy, and she had to defeat him first. But she used her cunning and he was easily dealt with. Once he was out of the way, she set about her great work and began to extract the happiness from the land. She knew there'd be a hero or two on the way. There always is. But the only heroes her enemies could come up with were a weakling innocent baby," she tapped the top of the cage, "and his big sister, with her useless flailing fists. They were no match for this witch. She captured them both and continued to reap goodness, sunshine and joy from the land. On the day her victory was complete, she dined early on lightly boiled and fragrant sweetmeats. Then she set off across the joy-mown land in triumph and all the people she had crushed bowed down before her. And for everyone except that wicked, *wicked* witch, it was a gloriously *unhappy* ending!"

She flapped her wings and flexed her claws. "The Land of Ever After will be mine – and what a wonderful world it will be. A world of sorrow and surrender. A world of endless night!"

"You'd like to see that, wouldn't you, Stark?" The witch poked the big man in the back. "You'd like to witness my moment of triumph. See how evil has ironed out good? What do you think? Shall I take you along for the ride?" She cackled until dark green spit came out of her mouth and dribbled down her chin.

Stark didn't respond. He turned and began to lumber slowly away.

"Oh, that's right, Stark," the witch called after him. "You've got work to do, haven't you? Press the tablecloth, Stark. Set out the silver. Polish the sharpest ivory forks. And," she snapped her fingers, "prepare the ebony bone cracker! Because tomorrow," she jumped to her feet and sneered down at Nettle and Wild, who were flinching below her, "TOMORROW," she screeched, "I DINE!"

Max tore his eyes from his spyhole and scrabbled quickly

away from the wall. He needed time to think and a safe place to do it in. If only Nettle hadn't been so impulsive, they could have worked out what to do together. That was Nettle, though, she never thought before she acted. And now she was paying the price. They all were. He'd got so used to having Nettle by his side. Now that she wasn't, it was like a part of him was missing.

He knew he had to go on, even if he was alone. It was down to him now.

And he did have one advantage. Thanks to Wild lumping his and Nettle's names together, Babs Haggard didn't know Max existed. He'd hated Wild doing that before, but he was grateful for it now. Babs Haggard didn't know about him and he had to keep it that way.

But where should he go now? Which door should he choose? He picked one at random and ran through it.

Straight into the man called Stark.

Chapter Seventeen

At once Max felt Stark's broad hand clamp around his mouth. He struggled and fought, but the big man trapped both his arms easily. He didn't even seem to notice the desperate kicks Max aimed at his knees.

Moving more quickly than Max had seen him move before, Stark carried Max into the centre of the black hall. He leaned over and lifted a circular trapdoor in the floor. He swung Max's feet over the dark opening and dropped him in.

Max imagined himself falling for hundreds of metres, into a pool full of crocodiles or a pit full of writhing snakes. But he landed almost immediately in a pile of straw. He leaped up, jumping wildly for the trapdoor. He could see Stark looking down at him, preparing to close the door. Was this the last light he would ever see? Would he be locked away down here until he starved to death?

"Please!" he cried. "Please let me up. Please don't do this!"

The big man paused and stared down at him steadily. He didn't answer, just crouched at the opening, looking down. Beneath his hooded grey eyelids Max saw that his irises were a faded bronze. There was something in his gaze that reminded Max of someone. He had no idea who. He hadn't met any people with bronze-coloured eyes. But maybe that little bit of colour left in the man meant there was still some goodness in him after all.

"Are you a prisoner here too?" Max remembered reading somewhere that if someone kidnapped you, you should try and get to know them so that they didn't treat you so badly. He spoke quickly. "Why are you working for her? Why do you want to do her dirty work? She's evil, but you don't have to be evil too. You could help me." He felt his voice rise in desperation. "Please help me." He began to shout but Stark stood up, the trapdoor clicked shut and Max was left alone in darkness.

As his eyes become accustomed to the dark, he saw he was in a dungeon, as dark and gloomy as the ones he remembered from his old story books. Water dripped down the walls. There was nothing in there but the heap of straw and an upturned metal bucket. There were no doors and no way up to the trapdoor above his head.

There was no way he could possibly get out.

He gave the bucket a sharp kick.

He'd come all this way. He'd escaped from a troll, he'd solved a maze, he'd found the Shining Pathway, he'd climbed a mountain he thought he never could climb, and survived a terrifying descent. And what had it all been for? Nothing. Because the minute he was on his own he'd let himself get caught by Babs Haggard's servant!

The bucket rolled away and clattered into the wall. Above it, high up, was a small arched opening, like a hole made by a large mouse.

Max righted the bucket and stepped up on it. Standing on tiptoe, he could just see out, his eyes level with the ground outside. He could see the cage in the courtyard and behind it the castle wall, with its weird collection of storm drains and gutters, all of it dusted with ash.

Babs Haggard was still standing on the cage. She rolled her black eyes and the chicken feet loomed into view. Max watched in horror as they shouldered the cauldron-chariot and placed it on a tripod over a big pile of wood and rubbish.

The witch raised her hands to the sky. As if to order, a black cloud formed above her. She clapped her hands and heavy rain poured into the cauldron. It rattled loudly on the iron base, and then more quietly as the cauldron began to fill. Babs Haggard stood very still, her palms pressed together in satisfaction as she watched her terrible cooking pot fill with water. Max couldn't pretend it was some nightmare, much as he wished it was. She really did intend to eat Wild. It was all over. None of them would ever get home.

"You can't do this!" Nettle was shouting and shaking the bars of the cage. "We won't let you do this!" Her eyes roved about and Max could tell she was looking for him, wondering where he was.

"Who's going to stop me, my darling?" Babs Haggard said.

"You don't need to know," Nettle replied. "Someone will, though. I'm telling you. They will!" Nettle may have run straight into the witch's trap but she wouldn't give Max away. Seeing the hope in her eyes, Max felt as if his stomach had been lined with heavy stones. Nettle didn't know he'd given himself away already, without any help from her.

"Oh, I hate to contradict you," the witch said, swaggering about on the cage, "but I don't think so. Oh, I'm going to love tomorrow. Very much." She stretched and flexed her fingers. "But to enjoy it to the full, I want to make sure I'm at my absolute best, or should I say, *worst*." She cackled horribly. "So I shall need a lovely long rest. And, do you know what? I think I'll sleep right here. You don't mind, do you, Maxi-Nettle? Hmm?"

She didn't wait for Nettle to answer but lay down on top

of the cage. Her black eyes swirled as she watched the rain still pouring steadily into the cauldron.

"The sweetest of sounds!" she breathed. "Better than any lullaby!" Her eyes slowly stopped swirling and, although they didn't close, Max could tell from the icy whistle that came from her rhythmically flaring nostrils that she was asleep.

Wild, exhausted by fear and too much gravy, laid his head in Nettle's lap and slept too. Nettle stayed sitting upright, stroking his hair.

"Nettle," Max dared to whisper after a time. "Over here!"

"Max!" Nettle looked about. "Where?" She couldn't see him at first so he stuck his fingers out of the hole and wiggled them at her.

Nettle's eyes lit up.

"How did you get down there? What are you going to do? How are you going to get us out?"

"I don't know," he whispered back. "Stark caught me. I'm trapped."

"What? You've been caught too?" Her face fell. The light in her eyes vanished as quickly as it had come. "Then this really is the end of the story."

"Don't say that," Max said. "We need to put our heads together, come up with a plan."

Nettle gave a bitter laugh. "What plan?" she hissed. "Don't you see, Max? There's no more time for plans. She's won. She's going to eat Wild in the morning, and me too probably. It's going to be just like Hansel and Gretel. Only in this version," she looked up at Babs Haggard's body, spread out on the cage above her like a giant crow, "in this version, the witch wins."

She dropped her head.

"Nettle." Max tried to get her attention again, but she turned her face away from him and buried it in Wild's hair.

Max had never seen Nettle look defeated. It shocked him. He'd expected her to have a go at him for getting himself caught. Tell him what a coward he was, what an idiot. This wasn't Nettle at all. The real Nettle was courageous and fierce; she wouldn't give in to anybody.

But she had now.

Max felt emotions racing and flickering through him like flames. Emotions that he'd never felt in his life before. He was full of hatred for Babs Haggard, full of anger at himself for getting caught, and full of fury at the injustice of this whole thing.

And that wasn't all. He felt a surge of determination rise up in him. A determination to make all this stop.

But what exactly could he do? He had no weapons. He couldn't stab Babs Haggard with the brooch because he'd left it with the gingerbread man. He couldn't strangle her with his cape either, because he'd left that behind too.

Desperately he turned out his pockets. There was nothing left except one marble, Wild's chewed crayon and Tilly the troll's juniper berries. He racked his brains. Bill Fairfoul had told him he was the chosen one because of what he'd said in the cake. But he was no expert on happy endings; he'd already proved that, several times. So there had to be more to it. If Bill was right and the Pool of Portent never lied, there had to be a real reason why it was him who was here, and not some junior superhero with outsize muscles. There had to be something he could do. Maybe something *only* he could do.

"Think, Max, think!" He talked to himself in a way that Nettle might have done a day ago. But he couldn't think of anything. It was pathetic!

In his frustration he reached through the opening and clutched a fistful of the ash which littered the courtyard. He squeezed it with all his strength. "Think! Think! Why me? Why is it me?"

When he opened his palm again, the ash, which was damp from Babs Haggard's rain shower, stayed in a tight ball. He opened his other hand, which still held Mum's last marble. It glimmered green and gold. It was probably the only bright thing left in Beyond. He stared out at Babs Haggard where she slept on the cage, guarding Nettle and Wild. He stared at her terrible cauldron as it filled with dark rainwater. And he stared at the black doughnut walls of her palace and the gutters and drains that coiled themselves around it like twisted snakes.

Max jumped down from the bucket. He buried the marble in the clump of ash he still held, and paced about his cell, throwing it up and catching it, over and over again. He had to find a way to defeat this witch. He had to. He had to be more cunning than she was. He had to be brave, and he had to beat her at her own game. If this was a story he was in, it wasn't just Babs Haggard's story. It was their story too. His and Nettle's. And Wild's.

"The story of Max and Nettle," he murmured, as he tossed the ash and the marble from hand to hand, "Max and Nettle. Max and Nettle and Wild."

And as the clump of ash slowly surrounded the marble and turned into a tight hard ball in his hands, so a plan finally began to form in his mind.

Chapter Eighteen

Max worked long into the evening. He worked as fast as he could. It was the only evening he had left and he was prepared to work all night if necessary.

Using Wild's stub of crayon, he scribbled notes and drew diagrams on the dungeon wall. He crossed to his tiny window many times, studying the layout of the courtyard and palace walls, gauging distances, estimating speeds.

Fortunately, the network of gutters and drains lit up as darkness came, shining as white as searchlights in a prison camp, and he had enough light inside his cell to see what he was doing. He jotted down sums, crossed out diagrams and started new ones, going over the details again and again until he was sure.

By the time it was properly dark he had filled every wall

of his cell, and Wild's crayon was no bigger than a headache tablet. He stood back, crumbling the last of the white wax in his fingers. He couldn't do any more drawings, but it didn't matter. He was satisfied with the final one.

He had a plan now. It might even work. But only if he could get out of the dungeon.

Hearing a rustling behind him, he turned to see movement in the straw.

Cautiously, he went over, and used his hands to pull apart the straw pile.

He jumped. A grey rat was there. The rat was as surprised as Max. Seeing him, it sat up and burrowed back into the straw, its wiry tail flicking as it disappeared.

The rat had been nibbling at a cloth bag. Max hadn't noticed that being there before. There was a hole in the bag and the corner of a hunk of bread was sticking out. Max's mouth watered. He was ravenous. Now that he thought about it, he hadn't had anything to eat since the previous night, at Loth's cottage. He didn't care if he was sharing it with a rat, he wanted that bread.

Lifting the bag out of the straw, he realised that it was tied at the top with a rope. A rope that dangled in the centre of his prison. He followed the rope upwards with his eyes.

The trapdoor was open!

Stark must have been back and lowered the bread bag down. Max had been so involved with his diagrams, he

186

hadn't even heard him. He didn't know why the man had given him food. Maybe he was going to be fattened up like Wild. He gnawed on the bread anyway – he was too hungry not to – and stared up at the opening where the trapdoor should be.

He yanked on the rope. It was firm. It must have been secured somehow in the hall above him. It was stupid of Stark to forget and leave it like that, Max thought. The rope was tough and thick, much stronger than you needed to lower and hoist a bag of bread. And why lower the bread down on a rope anyway? Why not just throw it in?

No, Stark had definitely left the rope and the open trapdoor on purpose. Was it a trap? Or was Stark giving him some kind of lifeline? Climbing up the rope was a risk, and not one the old Max would ever have considered. But he was different now.

He finished the bread and wiped his hands on his knickerbockers. Then he took one last look at his final diagram, memorising the details. He checked his pockets, took hold of the rope, and began to climb, hand over hand over hand.

He paused, clinging to the rope, as his head came up into the hall. He let himself spin round once in a circle, watching. There was no sign of Stark. The hall was deserted. He pulled himself out onto the cold floor. Moving as silently as possible, taking care not to let Snow White's boots tap too loudly on the hard marble, he made for the door to the courtyard.

Babs Haggard was still snoring on top of the cage. Nettle and Wild both seemed to be asleep too. The cauldron was full now and the rain had stopped. Max was worried about getting past the chicken feet but they didn't budge as he sidled by them.

Keeping low, he tiptoed round the back of the cage and crouched down. He glanced round for Stark. But there was no one else there. He touched Nettle gently on the shoulder.

She woke with a start. "Not yet!" she whimpered. "Not yet!" She must have been having a nightmare about what was meant to happen in the morning.

"Shh!" Max urged. "Quiet. We mustn't wake her."

"Max!" Nettle whispered. "How did you get out?" She peered up at the shadowy figure of the witch above her. "You'd better run. Get away while you still can. Save yourself."

"I'm going to save *you*!" Max said. "You and Wild."

"Not possible." Nettle stroked Wild's hair, gently unwinding a curly lock and then letting it spring back to the little boy's sleeping head. "It's too late for us."

She turned away as if that was the end of the conversation.

"It's not too late!" Max hissed. "We can still stop her. Never say never!"

"Those are just words, Max," Nettle said in her newly

dull voice. "They aren't going to do you any good."

"No? Maybe not. But I've thought of something that will." He edged closer to her. "Nettle, I've realised why I'm here. It's not because I'm an expert at happy endings, because I'm not. And it's not to do with being a fighter, or a climber, because I'm no good at them either. It's something else, something I'm really good at. Something only I can do!"

Nettle was still looking at Wild. She gave a small smile as if to say she was happy for Max, but that it really had nothing whatsoever to do with her.

"Listen to me, Nettle." Max took hold of the bars of the cage. "Babs Haggard is not going to win. She's not going to get her ending. Because I'm not going to let her!"

Nettle raised her head just a little, so he went on quickly, "But I'm going to need your help. You have to listen to me, OK? And, for once, you have to do exactly what I say."

She looked straight at him then, and although her expression was still one of defeat, he thought he saw a glimmer of hope return to her eyes.

"Tell me," she said.

Chapter Nineteen

Max was relieved to see the dwindling sun ease up over the horizon. He willed it on as it edged its way slowly upwards, then stayed low, drooping. It had done all it could do. The last morning had broken. Max knew he didn't have long to wait.

He hadn't slept at all. He'd spent the rest of the night going over his plan, doing and redoing the maths. He was stiff from spending hours crouched in his new hiding place, in the top of a storm drain on the palace wall. He'd had to squeeze through drains, crawl along gutters, shimmy up ramps and, worst of all, haul himself over a water wheel to get there.

But he'd reached the storm drain safely. Phase one of his plan was complete. Everything depended on what happened next. Despite his efforts to stop them, his legs jiggled constantly. The moment of truth was coming very soon, and his whole body knew it.

Sure enough, there were soon sounds of activity from the ground below.

"Oh, what a beautiful morning!" Max heard Babs Haggard say, although there was nothing beautiful about it. Looking down through the murk, he saw her sitting up on the cage and stretching.

"Wake up, my savoury dumpling," she said, poking Wild with her knitting-needle fingers.

"Wakey wakey, my sweet apple flummery!" She poked Nettle too, who grabbed Wild and pulled him away into the corner of the cage.

"Don't be shy, my pretty little teacakes!"

The witch laughed out loud, revelling in their distress.

She swivelled her eyes and Max saw the chicken feet come to life and transform, in an instant, into black dragons. He swallowed nervously. He thought he had a pretty good idea of what was likely to happen this morning, but he hadn't been anticipating dragons.

One by one the creatures breathed great orange blasts of fire onto the woodpile beneath the cauldron. From his position Max had a perfect view of the water inside the giant pot. In almost no time it came to a fast, rolling boil. Even high up on the wall, Max could feel the heat of it.

Babs Haggard clapped her hands and her wings.

"Time to prepare the ingredients!"

She swooped to the ground and ripped open the cage door, yanking Nettle and Wild outside into the open.

"Now then, Maxi-Nettle, my dear," Babs Haggard simpered at Nettle. "Time for you to see if the water's ready!"

Max tried to steady his breathing. He'd been expecting this, banking on it even, but that didn't make it any easier to watch.

The dragons leaned their scaly, armoured shoulders against the cauldron, making themselves into a sort of ladder; just as, when they were sugar mice, they had made a ladder for Wild to climb the toffee apple.

"Quick, quick, child. This way." Babs Haggard gestured for Nettle to go up the ladder, as casually as if she was inviting her to sit down in a comfy chair.

"I can't go up there, I'm afraid," Nettle said, exactly as she and Max had planned. "I'm scared of heights. Hadn't you better test the water yourself?"

"Pah!" exclaimed the witch. "That's the oldest trick in the book! Think I'm falling for that, do you? Well, I'm not." She clacked her hands together. "Now get up that ladder!"

Nettle took a step forward but Wild hung on to her leg. Max watched her bend and whisper to him. Gently, she released her leg from his arms. She held on to his hands for a moment and then put them by his sides. The little boy's mouth opened in a silent cry. Poor Wild, Max thought. He didn't know anything about the rescue plan. They'd decided it was too risky to tell him.

Keeping herself very straight, like a queen on the way to the gallows, Nettle left Wild and walked to the living ladder. She mounted the first dragon's back.

"Up! Up!" Babs Haggard screeched. Max could tell she was impatient to get things started. She believed this was her great morning. He hoped he could prove her wrong.

Obediently, Nettle climbed onto the second dragon.

"Higher!"

Again Nettle did as the witch demanded. Now she was standing on the back of the topmost dragon, dangerously near to the throbbing, steamy water. Max's own eyes stung as he imagined the appalling heat on her face.

"DOUSE HER!"

With a click from Babs Haggard's spiny fingers, the dragons opened their wings, preparing to lift off and fling Nettle into the pot.

"Wait!" Nettle shouted, struggling to keep her footing. "Wait. Haven't you forgotten something?"

"I don't think so, my honey cake," Babs Haggard snarled. "What could I possibly have forgotten? I've planned this breakfast down to the last detail!" She gestured to a little table Max hadn't noticed before. It had been set very elaborately for one. "It will be perfect! Won't it, Stark? You're looking forward to it, aren't you?"

Stark was standing in an alcove in the wall. He was so still Max hadn't even realised he was there. He didn't react to the witch's words, just stared out straight ahead like a guard in a sentry box.

"A perfect meal? But that's just it," Nettle said. She was doing brilliantly, Max thought. She'd nearly been plunged into a pot of scalding water but she was as cool as a cucumber. "You want this to go down in history, don't you? As the most triumphant meal ever? But how can it do that if the recipe isn't up to scratch?"

"Not up to scratch?" Babs Haggard flickered her hands in the air. "Whatever do you mean, girl?"

"Well, everyone knows that you can't make a top-quality human stew without the right spice. I'm good at cooking and recipes. I'll give you a tip if you like."

"Tip? Tip? What tip?" The witch was suspicious, but Max could tell Nettle had caught her attention. He dug his nails into the palm of his hand, praying that she would take the bait.

"For a truly delicious child stew," Nettle said, "you'll need to start with an excellent stock in your stockpot. And for an excellent stock, you'll need juniper berries. Flavour this lovely steaming water with juniper, and you'll have a dish fit for a witch queen. A dish to really go down in history."

The witch folded her arms.

"Hmm. And where would I find juniper berries, may I ask?"

"Up there." Nettle pointed upwards. "I've seen some on the wall."

"You're lying," Babs Haggard said. "Nothing grows in Beyond. I like it that way. Where would juniper berries come from?"

"I don't know. But they're there. I've seen them with my own eyes. A bird must have dropped them."

"What bird? There are no birds here."

"I don't know what bird," Nettle answered. "That's not my business. But the juniper berries are there all right. On that ledge. Go up and see for yourself if you don't believe me."

The witch peered at the wall. She looked back at Nettle.

"Juniper? A delicacy, you say?"

"King of all flavours," Nettle said.

"Wait right there!" Babs Haggard hitched up her skirts. With the help of her buzzing wings, she began to climb. She reached the ledge and bent over, sniffing, searching for the berries Max had put there on his way up.

Max took a deep breath. This was it. Nettle had played her part brilliantly. Now it was his turn.

Quickly he took out his last marble. He blew on it, placed it in the damp ash at the head of the drain and prepared to flick it. He couldn't start yet, though. The witch was hunched over the juniper berries, scrabbling about greedily, trying to make sure she got every last one for her horrible stockpot. His plan wouldn't work with her like that. He needed to get her to stand up.

"Hey! Babs Haggard!" he shouted. "There are more berries up here!" Keeping one hand on the marble, he waved his free arm so that the short-sighted witch would be able to see him.

"Maxi!" Wild shouted. "Maxi!"

The witch straightened her back. "What! Who's that? Who are you? I wasn't expecting you. Where did you come from? Stark!" she demanded, jerking her head from side to side. "Did you know about this intruder? What is the meaning of this? Who are you, boy?"

She hitched her skirts and flapped her wings, preparing to advance up the guttering in front of her.

"I'm Max," Max said loudly, stopping her in her tracks. "I've come to defeat you. I've come to save Wild and Nettle, and bring back colour and happiness to the land. I'm doing it right now!"

He gave the marble a sharp flick.

He watched out of the corner of his eye as it trickled round and round the head of the drain and then began to roll away, gathering speed and ash as it went.

"You mean there are three of you?" Babs Haggard relaxed

again, folding her arms and cackling. "Three little children? And you were the best they could find? A baby, a girl and a puny little drumstick like you?" She stared at Max and scratched at her elbows as if she'd like to be scratching him.

"I may be puny," Max said, "but I'm very good at building marble runs. An expert, in fact. I know exactly how they work." He watched as the marble, now covered in so much ash it was the size of a cricket ball, rolled out of the storm drain and landed in the next section of gutter.

"What are you talking about?" the witch scoffed. "Marble runs? Toys! Come down here at once, boy. You're skin and bone, but you may as well go in the pot with the others. I'll have you for starters."

Max could hear the ball of ash rumbling down and up a U-shaped pipe, rushing along on the journey he had prescribed for it. The whooshing sound it made as it charged through the witch's outdoor plumbing system gave him confidence. His plan was working.

"You're not having a starter," he shouted down at her. "But you wanted an ending, didn't you? Well, now you're going to get one!"

The witch looked at him, flexing her metal fingers as if she would like to tear him to shreds. She began to climb towards him but his weapon, the ball of ash as big as a basketball now, with his last precious marble at its centre, was rumbling through the pipework. It was almost there. He willed it forward as it rumbled louder. It needed to hit her before she could get to him. It would, too, he told himself. It would smash into her at any moment.

Then, quite suddenly, the rumbling stopped. An eerie silence fell on the courtyard. Max froze and stared down in horror, realising that the ball wasn't moving any longer. The marble had grown as he'd meant it to, but now it was *too* big. It was stuck in the pipe. He must have miscalculated. His plan had failed.

Babs Haggard's eyes swirled in her head. A slow and awful smile appeared on her face.

"Something wrong, little boy?" she said.

Chapter Twenty

"Max?" Nettle called out from the topmost dragon, steam billowing around her. "What's happening? What is it?"

He looked at her in dismay. What could he say? That his plan had failed? That she and Wild would surely be eaten now, that none of them would ever see home or their parents again?

They'd been through so much and it had all been for nothing. Bill Fairfoul had been wrong about him after all. He was no saviour. The Land of Ever After would be destroyed and the three of them with it. Oddly, although he was terribly afraid, all he could think, as he closed his eyes and waited for whatever his fate would be, was that it was a shame he would never get to know Nettle and Wild properly. He would have liked to spend time with them in the real world, doing ordinary things. Now he'd never have the chance.

"Clattering clobberjays!" A voice resounded in the courtyard. "What, in the name of Ever After is going on here?"

Max opened his eyes again.

He wondered if he was dreaming as a white horse galloped through the open door of the hallway and reared up, whinnying.

A knight was riding the horse. A knight covered in grey mud, his clanking armour more tarnished and rusty than ever. He waved his lance cheerfully at Max.

"Sir Gladalad!" Max cried. "You came!" Maybe there was still hope for them after all.

"Halloo! Found ye at last, squire," the knight called back, reining Nobility in. "Been thinkin' 'bout what you said regarding the rainbows. Decided you had a point. Decided to give 'em a miss and see how you were all faring instead." He cast an eye around the courtyard, taking in Wild where he cowered on the ground beneath the cauldron, and Nettle, balanced precariously on the tower of dragons. "Not too well, I see. Hope I'm not too late. Been riding a day and a night. Had to come the long way round, via the foothills. Terrible maze there was, had to ride Nobility here on top of the thing, over the hedges, don't ye —"

"SILEEENCE!" The witch's scream was deafening. It

200

even stopped Sir Gladalad in his tracks. He gaped at her as she shrieked, "What are you doing here, you idiotic man? How dare you! I'll teach you to meddle in my affairs." She directed an arm at the dragons. "ATTACK!" she yelled. "ATTACK HIIIIM!"

The dragons flapped and beat their wings, and took off into the air. Nettle was still stranded on the top one.

"Look out!" Max called to her in panic, as she flung out her hands and tried desperately to keep her balance, like a novice on a surfboard. She looked helplessly in his direction as she passed and then toppled towards him.

Max's heart leaped. Just as he thought Nettle would fall with a smash into the courtyard, she landed heavily on the wall directly above him. She started to slide down, scrabbling for footholds. Without thinking, Max threw himself over her back, stopping her fall.

"Got you!" he said, hardly sure whether it was true. "I've got you!"

They lay, clinging together, watching, as the dragons circled Sir Gladalad.

"Why, by all that's unholy!" the knight said to Babs Haggard. "Here's a set of discourteous and frankly unattractive beasts."

Babs Haggard snarled.

"Retreat, I say," Sir Gladalad addressed the dragons. "Retreat at once, or face the consequences!"

The dragons waved their heads. Threatening growls came from deep in their scaly throats. They circled even closer.

Sir Gladalad dropped from his horse. "Well, don't say ye haven't been warned."

He drew a very rusty sword from the scabbard at his side and waved it so wildly round his head that Max worried he might accidentally cut it off.

"Have at thee, ye jumped-up newts!" he boomed as the dragons flew at him. Teeth snapping, breathing black fire, they yanked at his armour, wrenching it away, sinking sharp claws into the soft flesh they uncovered.

Sir Gladalad didn't seem a bit afraid. "Take your punishment!" he shouted from the fray. He began stabbing at the creatures, but it looked to Max as though the dragons were punishing Sir Gladalad, rather than the other way around. For every strike he made with his sword, he suffered several deep bites, long claw slashes and quite a few searing burns.

Sir Gladalad was doomed. Max was sure of it. He could only look on, stricken, until he became aware of Nettle hissing in his ear.

"The marble!" she was saying. "Max! What about the marble?"

He shook his head. "It's stuck," he said. He felt dazed. "Stuck in the pipe . . . Didn't work."

"We've got to get it out then!" Nettle eased herself down

the wall. "Come on," she hissed back at him. "Help me shift it!"

He followed her, working his way down to where the fattened marble was wedged in a dented part of the pipe. He hadn't known about the dent, so he hadn't allowed for it in his calculations.

"Come on," Nettle said. "We'll push it out!"

They were dangerously close to the witch now. Max could see her wings and the back of her head vibrating with excitement as she watched her dragons tearing at Sir Gladalad's body.

"Push!" Nettle said. "Push!"

Max doubted it could do any good now, but he pushed anyway, all the time keeping an eye on Sir Gladalad. For a moment, the knight seemed to gain the upper hand as two of the dragons fell away from him and rolled belly-up on the ground, floundering.

"Push harder, Max! Push harder!"

Max tried to push, but the ashy ball wouldn't budge. He kept trying, but he couldn't tear his gaze away from Sir Gladalad.

The third dragon was the strongest. It ripped Sir Gladalad's sword from his grasp with its teeth, then stood on its hind legs and placed its great front feet on the knight's broad chest, hooking in its claws. Sir Gladalad clutched at the feet and the two of them spun round together like drunken dancers until, with an almighty effort, Sir Gladalad managed to get his hands under the beast's shoulders and fling it away. It hit the wall and crashed to the ground.

The three battered dragons limped towards one another. They gathered together, heads touching. Suddenly they weren't dragons any longer. They were chicken feet again. Bloodied and bruised chicken feet.

Sir Gladalad batted at his moustache, which Max was alarmed to see was now on fire.

"That'll teach ye crusted witch's creations!" he said, brushing his gloved hands together, shaking off blood. He was staggering slightly as he mumbled, "Not a drop of common courtesy between you. No idea of how to . . . Wash me hands, I will . . . wash me hands of all . . . the lot of ye!"

He teetered to one side, dropped to the ground and lay still.

"Sir Gladalad!" Max cried.

Babs Haggard burst out laughing. It was such an evil laugh, so full of wickedness. Max hated her for it. Sir Gladalad was a good man. He had come all this way to help them and the witch had killed him, just like that. Max hated her so much. He hated her with a vengeance.

He leaned with all his might on the ash ball, with the marble at its centre. "Push, Nettle! Push!"

"That's what I've been telling you!" Next to him, Nettle grunted with effort.

The witch turned on them. "What are you two playing at?" she said, as Max, strengthened by sheer hatred, felt the ash ball give a little under his hands. "Enough of your games. Can't you see? It's all over for you now." She took a step towards them. Max and Nettle pushed again, even harder than before. "Come now, children," the witch hissed. "Come to—"

She didn't finish her sentence. A look of shock passed over her face as a giant ash boulder shot out of the drain, spun twice round a water wheel and blasted into her stomach.

The boulder swept her off the palace wall, propelled her through the air and threw her straight into her own cauldron.

She opened her mouth but didn't even have time to scream before she was plunged under the boiling water.

And she stayed under. Sizzling.

⚬⚬⚬ Chapter Twenty-One ⚬⚬⚬

Max, Nettle and Wild all stayed exactly where they were, keeping perfectly still until the sizzling stopped at last. The water in the cauldron, blackish grey now and thickened with ash, gave a couple of explosive glugs, shivered and went still.

The chicken feet clustered together, scratching uncertainly at the ground. Without Babs Haggard to command them, they seemed to be at a total loss. They pressed themselves against the cauldron and bobbed up and down harmlessly.

Max took in a huge gulp of air. He hadn't even realised he'd been holding his breath.

"Is Old Bag Haggard dead?" Wild gazed up with round eyes.

Nettle clambered quickly down the wall towards him.

"Definitely dead," she said.

"Definitely, definitely," said Max, following her, shimmying quickly through the drains. Despite the glitch in the pipe, the ash boulder had still been heavy enough and forceful enough to do its job. Thank goodness they had been able to get it going again. He felt immensely relieved.

He jumped to the ground, where he found himself being hugged enthusiastically by both Nettle and Wild.

As they embraced, the deep grey sky above them rolled back and was replaced by a bolt of blue, shot through with sunlight.

"You did it, Max!" Nettle said. "You did it! You defeated the witch! You've saved the Land of Ever After!"

"*We* did it, you mean," Max laughed with relief, hardly daring to believe it. "I couldn't have done it without you, Nettle. You were really brave. But then you always are."

"And you were really, really clever. I've got to say it, Max. I reckon you're a genius!"

"Genius!" repeated Wild, wrapping himself firmly round Max's legs. Max couldn't believe his ears. He never thought he'd hear Nettle pay him a compliment. He felt pride swell in his chest.

A deep sigh came from behind him.

He whirled round. "Sir Gladalad!"

The knight lay on the ground, his eyelids flickering. He wasn't dead. Or at least, not quite.

Nettle and Max rushed over to him. Hastily, Nettle took off her jacket and used it to kill the fire that still smouldered in his moustache.

"Let's try to give him some air."

As gently as she could, she eased off Sir Gladalad's helmet. Max helped her strip him of what was left of his body armour. There was blood everywhere. A worrying amount.

Together they lifted Sir Gladalad's shoulders and worked Nettle's jacket under his back. Nettle tied the sleeves at the front, knotting them together as tightly as she could to stop the wounds from bubbling out more blood.

"That'll hold for now, I think." She looked at Max. They could both see it was useless. They couldn't save Sir Gladalad's life by themselves. The knight needed urgent medical attention. His bravery had bought them the time they needed. He was a hero, and they couldn't let him die. But where could they get help from?

"Bill Fairfoul!" Max said after a moment, remembering how the wolf had miraculously cured his cut ankle. Maybe he could heal mortal wounds too. It was their only chance.

"OK," Nettle said. "Let's try and get him on his horse."

As if he understood what was required, Nobility clopped towards them.

"Nay. Don't bother with me, young adventurers," Sir Gladalad said huskily, coming to. "Leave me to the termites." He gazed up at the sky. *"Here lies Sir Gladalad Gadabout.*

Wasted his time tilting at tricks of the light. Tell them to put that on me headstone, if they can be bothered."

"You're not going to die, you silly man!" Nettle told him. But looking at the knight's ghostly pallor, and given the journey that still awaited them, Max wasn't so sure.

"Not afraid to go," Sir Gladalad continued faintly. "Only wish I could have set eyes on my fair Willamina just one more time. Dash it all. Can't be helped."

Nobility bent down to his master, nuzzled his hair and whickered gently.

"Stop talking about dying!" Max said, grunting with effort, as the three of them tried and failed to drag him onto his horse. "We're going to get you to Happy End and the wolf's going to make you better."

"No, no." Sir Gladalad's head rolled. "Can't go to Happy End. Been banished . . . 'Gainst Lord Malberry's wishes. I never did show that thing he wanted me to show, that what-do-you-me-call-it. That . . . what was it again? True something, true . . . true . . . ."

His eye glazed over and he flopped to the side in a dead faint.

"True mettle."

It wasn't Max who said the words. It wasn't Nettle, and it wasn't Wild either.

Max had forgotten about Stark. They all had.

"True mettle," he said again. He coughed, and his voice

was wheezy and cracked, as if he hadn't spoken for a very long time. "He has shown true mettle."

"You!" Nettle exclaimed. Instinctively, she reached for Wild and pulled him to her. "Stay where you are. Don't you come near us!"

"Wait," Max said, watching the big man blinking at Nettle, flinching at her words as if they were blows. "I don't think he means us any harm. We could use his help."

"No, Max," Nettle said. "He's evil. He was going to let us all die!"

"At least let him help us get Sir Gladalad on his horse. We can't do it by ourselves."

Nettle kept her eyes fixed suspiciously on Stark. "All right," she said. "But that's all."

Going closer, Max saw that Stark had chains around his ankles. He was shackled to the wall of his alcove.

"You're a prisoner here, too, aren't you?" he said.

A padlock with a key in it was secured to the wall, out of Stark's reach. The alcove was a perfect vantage point from which to see everything that happened in the courtyard. It looked as if the witch had placed Stark there deliberately.

"She wanted you to watch, didn't she?" Max said as it came to him. "But why? Who *are* you?"

Stark didn't reply, but Max thought he saw a look of anguish cross his stony face.

Max couldn't quite make sense of it, but something was

coming together in his mind. He turned the key in the padlock and beckoned Stark forward. "Help us here!" he said.

Nettle kept a protective arm round Wild as Stark lifted Sir Gladalad and gently laid his limp body across the saddle.

"Now let's go!" Nettle said, taking Wild's hand and grabbing Nobility's bridle.

"Wait!" Max was still puzzling over Stark. "I think he should come with us."

"What?" Nettle was outraged. "No way!" Max felt her cold glare on him. "Why? We should leave him here to rot. He's as bad as the witch."

"I'm not sure about that."

Max approached Stark and tried to look into his averted eyes. "You could have told Babs Haggard about me, couldn't you? But you didn't. You protected me from her. You left the trapdoor open for me on purpose."

Stark blinked his bronze eyes and licked his dry, scabby lips.

"Stop wasting time, Max. He's not worth it." Nettle was eager to be away.

"I don't know who you are, or what your story is," Max said to Stark. "But I do know you're not all bad." Whoever the man was, he couldn't leave him alone in Beyond. It wouldn't be right. He put out a hand. "Come on. You're coming with us."

"It's a mistake," Nettle grumbled. But she didn't say any more as she led Nobility away.

"Come on," Max said again, turning to leave. Stark hesitated. Then, keeping his head lowered, he began to shamble slowly after him.

As they went through the hall, Max heard a huge creaking sound. Looking up, he saw the ceiling was caving in and set to fall.

"Quickly!" he shouted. They rushed out of the front door and made for the iron gates. Once he was sure they were all through, Max looked back and saw that Babs Haggard's palace was buckling and bending. Drains and gutters snapped and fell. The whole place was collapsing.

To Max's astonishment, the chicken feet staggered out of the palace after them. They rushed up to him and bobbed around him. He tried to shoo them away, but each time he did, the chicken feet took a few uncertain steps backwards and then began to follow again, as if they were his loyal dogs.

Max decided to ignore them for the time being. There were more important matters to consider.

As they hurried towards the maze, he worried about how they would ever pass its ash-filled paths. He was afraid they would have to dig their way out, and judging from the way Sir Gladalad looked – still out cold, arms dangling – they really didn't have time for that.

But as they approached the entrance and he touched the

first steely black hedge, the ash flew up and revealed the first of Max's marbles, shining in the sunlight. Wild picked it up and held it out. "Here's your marble, Maxi."

"Nah," said Max. "It's OK. You found it. You keep it."

He wasn't worried about the marbles any longer. And he liked seeing the look on Wild's face each time he discovered another one of them. The little boy looked more like himself now. He ran ahead gathering all the other marbles, and very soon they were out the other side of the maze and staring at a girl Max had never seen before.

She was kneeling by the yellow cape that still covered the gingerbread man. She was digging a little hole near his head and planting bright blue flowers. The blue of the flowers was so deep, so intense, that Max thought they were the most gorgeous thing he'd ever seen. But even more remarkable than the flowers was the girl's red hair. Metres and metres of it flowed out behind her like a calm river.

"Told you you'd be back," she said.

"Rapunzel!" Nettle exclaimed.

Of course it was Rapunzel, Max realised. Her skin was smooth as cream and her hair the colour of ripe strawberries, but her cheery voice was just the same.

"But how did you get down here?" Max said.

"Easy," Rapunzel answered. "My prison window fell out. It must have happened the moment you killed the witch. You have killed the witch, haven't you?"

213

Max nodded, remembering the sizzling cauldron.

"Knew it. I came straight up to the mountain top and slid down the stack to meet you. And look what I found."

She gestured towards the mountain. An arch had opened up in the rock, and behind it was a tunnel, filled with welcoming golden light.

"Looks like your journey back to Happy End's going to be a piece of cake," Rapunzel said. "Mind if I join you?"

Chapter Twenty-Two

Rapunzel was right. The journey back to Happy End was easy. And if Max hadn't been so worried about Sir Gladalad it would also have been the most amazing journey ever.

As soon as they came out of the tunnel, the barren grey landscape they had left behind on the other side of Harsh Mountain began to change. As Max and Nettle and Wild led the way, the earth transformed beneath their feet. Grass sprouted, leaves unfurled, and flowers spread out their petals. They walked on a carpet of flowers which seemed to unroll under their feet: yellow buttercups, white daisies and pink clover, all humming with the sound of busy insects and bees, alive with the fluttering of butterflies. Birds sang and swooped, gliding through the expanding blue of the now cloudless sky. Apple trees that had been as good as dead came into leaf again and filled with ripe red apples, ready to harvest. They picked as many as they wanted and walked along munching. The crisp juicy fruit tasted fantastic.

As they walked they were joined by people they had met along the way. The three little pigs popped out from rocks behind which they had been hiding. Thumbelina flitted by on her swallow, whooping as she looped the loop over their heads.

Pinocchio came, walking hand in hand with an old man wearing a carpenter's apron.

"Look," Pinocchio said to Max, his nose as neat and small as a button. "I found my papa who loves me. And I love him." He rubbed his nose happily.

"That's good," Max said, feeling a pang of envy as Pinocchio and Gepetto fell in behind them. "I'm hoping to find my dad soon, too." Life in Mansley seemed such a long way away now. So much had happened, it was hard to imagine himself back there.

They did have one setback. When they reached the river, Tilly the troll stamped her big tree-trunk legs apart, blocking the bridge.

"Where's my billy goat?" she demanded, folding her arms emphatically across her chest. There was no way she was going to let Max across this time.

"Ah," Max said. "Tilly. Hi!" He felt in his pockets. They

were completely empty. He didn't have so much as a peace offering for the troll, let alone a billy goat.

"You hasn't forgotten, has you?" Tilly frowned suspiciously. "You pinky promised me, you did."

"No. No of course I haven't forgotten."

Although he had. Max didn't know what to do. He was relieved when Nettle came alongside him.

"Tilly," she said gently. "Have you ever *seen* a billy goat? Do you know what a billy goat looks like?" Max remembered that Tilly was a little hazy on this, since she had mistaken *him* for a billy goat before.

Tilly looked furtive, as if she thought Nettle was trying to catch her out. "Not exactly *seen*," she said. "But I knows they're living creatures. They're about so big." She held air the size of a large dog in her hands. "I'll know one when I sees one!"

"That's right!" Nettle said. "Billy goats are just that size, aren't they, Max?" She nodded to him meaningfully.

Suddenly Max understood what she was planning.

"Yes, yes, they are." It was a brilliant idea of Nettle's. It might just work too.

Max put his fingers in his mouth and whistled. It was a really good whistle. He'd never managed one so sharp and loud before. Tony and Rio would have been impressed. He hadn't thought about them for ages, but it crossed his mind that he didn't care one bit about impressing them any more.

217

The chicken feet scurried forward, scrambling to be the first to reach Max. They seemed to regard him as their master now and were eager to do his bidding.

"Hey, Tilly," Max said. "How would you like *three* billy goats?"

Tilly clapped her hands together under her chin. "Three! Ooh! I would like three. I would, yes!"

"Go!" Max commanded. Dutifully, the feet hurried towards Tilly, who scooped them up in her strong arms.

"Three lovely billy goats!" she exclaimed. "Now I is the happiest troll alive. They is beautiful!"

"Are you going to eat them?" Wild asked her, trotting across the bridge. He was fascinated. He hadn't met a troll before.

Tilly chortled. "'Course not. I only eats fish. I don't want billy goats to *eat*. I wants them to play with!" She chuckled as she began to juggle the feet, occasionally dropping one when she tossed it too high.

"Ooch!" Nettle whispered to Max. "Do you think they're enjoying that?"

Max shrugged. "I guess it'll keep them busy. Anyway, it's better than running around after me all day like . . . like headless chicken feet!"

Nettle laughed a husky laugh. Max didn't think he'd ever heard her laugh properly before. He made a mental note to try and make her do it again.

The flowing of the river seemed to rush them on and Max stepped up the pace. He hadn't forgotten that Sir Gladalad was still unconscious and needed urgent attention. He strode on faster and the band of people behind him walked faster too.

They must be quite a sight, he thought, as he looked back at the growing parade behind him. Nettle, leading Nobility and chatting to Rapunzel. The three little pigs carrying Rapunzel's hair as if it was the train of a red wedding dress. Gepetto, arm in arm with Pinocchio. Tilly, juggling her chicken feet billy goats, with Wild running along beside her. Other people kept joining them too – some of them he recognised, some he couldn't place, but they all seemed happy and excited to be on the journey. All except for Stark, who kept his distance from everybody, hunched and limping, bringing up the rear.

One person who hadn't joined them was Loth. Max imagined him, still shut up alone in his cottage at the bottom of the mountain. He shivered. He was so glad he hadn't stayed there. It was hard to believe he'd even been tempted. Loth had said they were alike. But Max knew now that he was nothing like Loth. He didn't want to stay shut up on his own. He had things to see. Places to go. At least he did – as long as he could get home.

He was thinking about Dad again when Nettle grabbed his arm and pulled him to a stop.

"Look," she said.

"Wolfie!" Wild shouted and ran towards the tall figure of Bill Fairfoul, who was standing like a lookout on top of a hill. It took Max a moment to realise that the hill was Giant Fell, and that they were back at Happy End. Giant Fell was almost unrecognisable now. It was totally covered in lush green moss and thick purplish heather. The raised fist Max had seen from Harsh Mountain and mistaken for a tree really was a tree now, full of pink cherry blossom, rich with sweet scent. Only the shape of the hill, along with its name, hinted at what it once had been.

"Max," said the wolf. "You did it. You killed Babs Haggard. You have broken her every spell. I am indebted to you. We all are."

Behind him, a crowd of people and animals grouped together. Among them, Max spotted Snow White and the dwarves, looking at him curiously. Red and her grandma were there too. And Aurora and Prince Casper, Jack and his mother. They looked peaceful and happy, and their clothes were all colourful again, bright as a picture book.

"Thanks very much," they said. "We appreciate it. Don't know what we would have done without you."

"You're welcome," Max said, feeling proud but embarrassed too. "And it wasn't just me. I had a lot of help." He smiled at Nettle. "But please, we need *your* help now. There's an emergency. Can you help us, Bill?"

Nettle led Nobility forward. The horse turned to the side and revealed Sir Gladalad's limp body, still flung across the saddle.

Bill Fairfoul stared. He seemed oddly reluctant to come forward.

"Please," Nettle said. "Sir Gladalad needs you. He saved our lives and risked his own. We're worried he may not have long to live."

The wolf seemed to shake himself then, and he padded forward to examine the knight. Max noticed that his paws were trembling as he touched the blood-stained bandages.

"I do not have the strength for this." The wolf sounded properly upset. Max was surprised. Bill Fairfoul was always so still and strong – nothing could shake him. But this had.

"I know that voice." Sir Gladalad's eyes fluttered open. "Bill? Bill, my darling girl. Is that you?"

"He's got a fever, I'm afraid," Nettle explained. "He might not be quite in his right mind."

"Know those eyes anywhere," Sir Gladalad went on. "Clear as warmest amber."

A tear fell from one of Bill Fairfoul's bronze-coloured eyes. "Glad," he whispered. "Glad."

"Hello, dearest," said Sir Gladalad. "Delighted to see you. Never thought to set eyes on you again. Though I'm blowed if I know why you've come as a wolf!"

Max said, "Hold on. Do you two know each other?"

"Know each other?" Sir Gladalad seemed to strengthen a little and he managed a weak guffaw. "We don't just know each other. We love each other, don't we, Willamina?"

"We do," the wolf's voice quivered.

"Wait," Max said, trying to understand. "You mean you're not a wolf really. You're not a man, either?"

"I know who you are!" Nettle exclaimed. "You're Lady Willamina Malberry!"

"I am," the wolf said softly.

The story characters looked shocked. They began bowing and curtseying. Max was pretty sure some of them were feeling guilty about the suspicious way they'd treated the wolf.

He was struggling to take in the news himself, and there was something he still didn't understand. "If you're really a girl, shouldn't you have changed back, now that the witch is dead? Like everything else?"

"This was not the witch's work," the wolf said. He, or rather *she*, as Max realised he would have to think of the wolf from now on, gestured at her long, furry body. "It was my father's doing."

"Blowed if I care what you look like," Sir Gladalad said, still hanging over his horse. "I want to marry you, Bill."

"Really?" Tears filled the wolf's eyes. "You mean it?"

"Of course. If we can't be man and wife, let's be man and wolf. It's all the same to me! Say ye will."

"I will," the wolf gasped. "As soon as you're better, I will!"

She hugged him and, despite his wounds, Sir Gladalad managed to hug her back.

Everyone else was so touched by the noble couple's reunion that they burst into a spontaneous round of applause. No one clapped louder than Max and Nettle.

The applause was interrupted by loud, heaving sobs.

Stark staggered out of the group and threw himself to his knees in front of the wolf.

"I'm so sorry!" he cried. "Never forgive me! You must never forgive me!"

The wolf, Lady Willamina, eased herself from Sir Gladalad's embrace. Slowly, she walked over to the stricken man and put her paw on his shuddering shoulder.

"I thought you were dead. I thought I'd never see you again. Where have you been, Father?"

Father? Max looked quickly at Nettle. Did this mean Stark was actually Lord Malberry? He was alive after all!

"In Beyond." Stark spoke through his sobs. "I've been in Beyond. Babs Haggard invited me there. She said we should pool our resources, share our power. We'd rule Ever After together, she said. She promised me a share of her strong magic. We'd have more power between us than people even dream of. And I . . . I was greedy enough to go."

"Who'd have thought Stark Malberry would let himself be tricked by a witch?" Jack's mother whispered loudly to Red's grandma.

Lord Malberry glanced up, his bronze eyes heavy with shame. Those eyes were just like Willamina's. Max knew they'd reminded him of someone. It had just never occurred to him that Stark could be related to a wolf.

"As soon as I arrived in Beyond she took everything I had," the miserable man went on. "All my magic. And she made me her slave. She didn't want to share with me. She didn't even want to rule the world herself. She wanted to crush it and everyone in it. She wanted hers to be the only story, and the last. She wanted to finish stories forever!

"I'm sorry, Willamina! I should never have gone. I should never have left you in this state. And now," he gripped her paw, "I have no magic. I no longer have the power to change you back!" He put his face to her large paw and its fur soaked up his tears.

"Then I am fated to be like this forever," Lady Willamina said sadly. "I'll be a mangy, foul-smelling wolf till kingdom come."

"Dashed if I care!" Sir Gladalad seemed to be rallying by the second. "I couldn't give a maggot! After all, what's a bit of a whiff between true lovers?"

"Hang on a minute," Nettle said. "Why do you think the magic is all gone? There's magic all around us. Max has brought it back. Can't you see? Max has the magic with him."

"Have I?" Max said. In his haste to get help for Sir

Gladalad he'd forgotten all about finding Lord Malberry's magic.

"Yes, of course." Nettle grinned at him. "Haven't you noticed, you dummy? Every time you take a step you bring back life and colour to the ground your foot touches. What's that if it isn't magic?"

Max looked around. He knew how much the landscape of Ever After had changed, but he didn't know that he was responsible for it. Glancing down, he saw the ground that surrounded his feet was shining like a halo round the moon.

The story characters nodded at what Nettle said, murmuring their agreement.

"So you should try touching Lady Willamina too," she went on. "If Stark can't change her back, maybe you can."

Max was going to protest but Nettle gave him a shove towards the wolf.

"Do the magic, Maxi," Wild said, jumping up and down in his nightie. "Do the magic!"

"Well, I'll have a go." Max stepped forward, feeling awkward as he realised that everyone's eyes were on him. "I'm not making any promises, though." He wiped his hands on his knickerbockers. "Shall we . . . shake hands or something?"

"Very well." Lady Willamina held out her paw and he took it. He touched the fur, leaping backwards as a clump of it came away in his fingers.

The wolf's body was clenching and unclenching, as if she was in terrible pain.

"Oh no! Sorry!" Max said. He was terrified that he'd hurt her very badly. But then, quite suddenly, the clenching stopped and the rest of the fur fell away. Bill straightened up.

She was still as tall, still as strong, still wearing the same trousers and top. She still had the same wise, bronze eyes, but she was a woman now. A really beautiful one, with no fur or tail but just a heavy brown plait that hung down her back.

"My own girl," sighed Sir Gladalad, who was looking much, much better.

"Thank you, Max," Lady Willamina said. She still had the same voice too; regal and wise and kind, all at once. "Thank you for turning me back into myself. Thank you for bringing my father back to me."

Stark bowed his head in shame.

"And above all, thank you for saving our happy endings."

Pinocchio ran forward and thrust a massive bunch of pink foxgloves at Max. There were so many, he must have been picking them all the way back to Happy End.

"Thank you, Max." Pinocchio gave a stiff little bow, and everyone else bowed too.

"We thank you," they said in unison.

"That's all right," Max said, feeling very pleased and a

little shy as he tried to see over the flowers. He almost added, "It was nothing," but stopped himself just in time. "I guess there'll be more stories in the Land of Ever After now, won't there? New ones, even."

"Lots of new ones," Lady Willamina agreed. "Thanks to you. What can we do for you in return, I wonder? Will you stay with us for a while, as our honoured guests? We'd be delighted to entertain you."

"Oh yes, do stay. Do!" the story characters cried.

"Can we, Maxi-Nettle? Can we?" Wild jumped around.

Max looked at Nettle and she smiled back at him. It was funny how they seemed to understand each other so much better now. In fact, they understood each other so well they sometimes didn't even need to say what they were thinking. Max had never experienced anything like that before.

"We'd love to stay," he began.

"We're really glad everything's straightened out," said Nettle.

"And it's great that you're you again, and you're all happy and everything, but . . ."

". . . the thing is," said Nettle, "we need to get back."

"Yes," said Max. "My sister and my little brother and I," he took Wild's hand in his and Nettle grinned at him, "we were at a wedding, you see. Quite an important one, actually."

"So we were wondering," said Nettle.

"If it's all right with you," said Max.

And then they both said together, "Could we have our cake back, please?"

Chapter Twenty-Three

Max loved every minute of the journey home. He didn't mind the dark this time. He didn't care how many times the cake bounced, or how fast it whirled. He squealed and whooped along with Wild, enjoying the roller-coaster feeling just as much as he did.

When the cake finally came to a halt, Max had no idea what they'd find. Would they be in the hotel? Would anyone else be there? Would the wedding celebrations have been over days ago, and the guests all gone home? Would Dad and Ilona be out looking for them?

When the lid began to slide away above their heads, he even half expected to see Lady Willamina standing there again, looking in.

"End of the road, guys!" a voice said and the lid came right off.

At once Max saw the streamers looping their way over the ceiling. He heard the excited hubbub in the room. He heard Dad laughing happily at something Ilona was saying, and he knew they were back in the hotel dining room.

"Off you go," said the waiter. "You're on!"

They hadn't missed anything. It was the very moment when they were supposed to pop up and shout, "We're all going to live happily ever after!"

Crouching in the cake, Max looked at Nettle and Wild. "Shall we?" he asked.

"Yes! Yes!" said Wild.

"Do it!" said Nettle.

Max and Nettle stood up on the piano stool, lifting Wild between them so he could see and be seen better.

"Here's to Ilona and Chris!" the three of them shouted. "Here's to all of us and our happy life together! Here's to the beginning of a brand-new story!"

Everyone clapped madly as they climbed out of the cake. Max ran to Dad, and Nettle and Wild ran to Ilona. They hugged their parents hard, as if they hadn't seen them for days – which, as far as they were concerned, they hadn't.

"Hello, lovelies," said Ilona. "That was brilliant! You changed the line, though. What happened to my Happily Ever After? Who made that decision?"

"We all did," said Nettle. "Actually, Mum, we made a lot of decisions when we were in that cake. Didn't we, Max?"

Max shrugged happily. "Did we?"

"Yes. Like, I decided I'm going to go to Max's school in September."

"Lovely!" said Ilona.

"Are you?" said Max. This was news to him.

"Yes," said Nettle. "I'm looking forward to it. I want to meet Tony and Rio. I think I'll enjoy that." She knitted her eyebrows together in a mock frown. Max chuckled as he realised he hadn't seen the real frown for quite some time. He thought he'd enjoy Nettle meeting Tony and Rio too. Now that he'd made a proper friend, he realised they needed putting in their places. And if anyone could do that, Nettle could.

"Me too!" Wild pulled at Ilona's dress. "I want to go to Maxi's school, too."

"You can," Ilona said. "You can start when Nettle does."

"And what about you, son?" Dad said. "Did you make any earth-shattering decisions in there? Anything I should know?"

Max grinned. Now that he thought about it, he realised he had made some decisions too.

"There are a couple of things, actually, Dad. I've decided

I don't need to bring my marble run with me to the new house. I think we should break it up. I can always start a new one, if I feel like it."

"Well, OK. If you're sure." Dad seemed quite relieved.

"I am." Max was surprised by how certain he felt about his decision. Along with Mum's marbles, the marble run had been the most precious thing in his life, but it just didn't seem so important now.

"Oh, and I think from now on, Dad, you're going to have to look after yourself a bit more, if you don't mind. Keep tabs on your inhaler and all that. Because I've got my own stuff to be getting on with."

Dad laughed and pulled Max to him. "I can see I'm going to have to be much more organised in future," he said.

Max looked at Ilona where she stood apart from him and Dad, hugging Nettle and Wild, and he had an idea.

He went back to the cake and collected the foxgloves Pinocchio had given him. He took them over to Ilona.

"These were my mum's favourite flowers," he said, as he held them out to her. "I thought maybe you might like them too."

It was probably the first properly friendly thing he'd ever said to Ilona. She looked as if she was going to cry.

"I love them," she managed to say. "I absolutely love them. Thank you, Max!" She grabbed him and hugged both him and the foxgloves to her.

"You're welcome," Max said, as he picked a strand of Ilona's hair out of her champagne glass.

"Thanks, Max," Dad said. His eyes were glistening too. "That means a lot."

"All right," Max said. "You don't have to cry about it. This is supposed to be a happy day, remember."

Dad and Ilona dabbed at their eyes and smiled through their tears.

Max felt a tug at his sleeve.

"I want to give *you* a present, too, Maxi," Wild said, looking up at him seriously.

Max picked him up and spun him round, pressing the little boy to his chest. "You already did. You gave me half a crayon, remember? It turned out to be the most useful half crayon in history."

Wild laughed gleefully as Max cuddled him and set him down again.

"What shall we do now, Maxi?" Wild said.

"Max." Nettle nudged him and he followed her gaze across the dining room to where the long doors stood open. The sun was coming out and the curtains wafted invitingly.

"Do you know what, Wild?" Max said. "I think we should go out. There's a whole world out there. I think we should go outside and explore."

"Good idea," said Nettle.

And Wild said, "Yay, Maxi-Nettle. Yay!"

Dodging between the tables, waving to the wedding guests, picking up bits of food as he went, Max ran, with Nettle and Wild jostling at his side. He ran as fast as he could, down the steps and right out into the garden.

Because he wanted to see what was out there.

He wanted to see how his new story would begin.